About Nicola Marsh

Nicola Marsh has always had a passion for writing and reading. As a youngster she devoured books when she should have been sleeping, and later kept a diary whose contents could be an epic in itself!

These days, when she's not enjoying life with her husband and sons in her home city of Melbourne, she's at her computer, creating the romances she loves in her dream job.

Visit Nicola's website at **www.nicolamarsh.com** for the latest news of her books.

Wedding Date with Mr Wrong

Nicola Marsh

First published in Great Britain 2012
by Mills & Boon, an imprint of Harlequin (UK) Limited.
Harlequin (UK) Limited, Eton House, 18-24 Paradise Road,
Richmond, Surrey TW9 1SR

© Nicola Marsh 2012

ISBN: 978 0 263 22816 8

Harlequin (UK) policy is to use papers that are natural, renewable
and recyclable products and made from wood grown in sustainable
forests. The logging and manufacturing process conform to the
legal environmental regulations of the country of origin.

Also by Nicola Marsh

Did you know these are also available as eBooks?
Visit www.millsandboon.co.uk

TM

CHAPTER ONE

'IF you mention weddings or tinsel or Secret Santa one more time I'm going to ram this wax down your throat.'

Archer Flett brandished his number-one-selling surf-board wax at his younger brother, Travis, who grinned and snatched the wax out of his hand.

'Resist all you like, bro, you know you're fighting a losing battle.' Trav smirked and rubbed a spot he'd missed on his prized board.

When it came to his family it always felt as if Archer was fighting a losing battle.

Despite making inroads with his brothers Tom and Trav, nothing had changed with his parents over the years—his dad in particular. That was why coming home for his yearly obligatory Christmas visit set him on edge. And why he rarely stuck around more than a few days.

This year would be no exception, despite Travis turning into a romantic schmuck.

'What were you thinking?' Archer stuck his board vertically in the sand and leaned on it. 'A Christmas wedding? Could you get any cheesier?'

His brother's eyes glazed over and Archer braced for some more claptrap involving his fiancée. 'Shelly wanted to be a Christmas bride and we saw no point in waiting.'

Archer placed his thumb in the middle of Trav's forehead and pushed. 'You're under this already. You know that, right?'

'We're in love.'

As if that excused his brother's sappy behaviour.

The Fletts were third-generation Torquay inhabitants, so he could just imagine the shindig his parents would throw for the wedding. The entire town would turn up.

Christmas and a wedding at home. A combination guaranteed to make him run as soon as the cake had been cut.

'You're too young to get married.' Archer glared at the sibling who'd tagged after him for years, pestering him to surf.

He'd spent the bulk of the last eight years away from home and in that time Travis had morphed from gangly kid to lean and mean. Heavy on the lean, light on the mean. Trav didn't have a nasty bone in his body, and the fact he was marrying at twenty-two didn't surprise Archer.

Trav was a marshmallow, and while Shelly seemed like a nice girl he couldn't imagine anything worse than being shackled to one person at such a young age.

Hell, at twenty-two *he'd* been travelling the world, surfing the hotspots, dating extensively and trying to put his folks' deception out of his mind.

A memory he'd long suppressed shimmered into his subconscious. South coast of Italy. Capri. Long hot nights filled with laughter and passion and heat.

Annoyingly, whenever anyone he knew was loco enough to tie the knot his mind drifted to Callie.

'So who're you bringing to the wedding?' Travis wrinkled his nose. 'Another of those high-maintenance city chicks you always bring home at Christmas?'

Archer chose those dates for a reason: women who demanded all his attention, so he didn't have time left over to spend one-on-one with his folks.

He'd honed avoidance to an art, ensuring he didn't say things he might regret. Like why the hell they hadn't trusted him to rally around all those years ago.

He wasn't the flighty, carefree surfer dude they'd assumed him to be and he'd prove it this trip. He hoped the surf school he'd developed would show them the type of guy he was—the type of guy he wanted to be.

'Leave my date to me.' He wriggled his board out of the sand and tucked it under his arm. 'Planning on standing here all day, gossiping like an old woman? Or are you going to back up some of your big talk by showing me a few moves out there?'

Trav cocked his thumb and forefinger and fired at him. 'I'm going to surf your show-pony ass into oblivion.'

'Like to see you try, pretty boy.'

Archer took off at a run, enjoying the hot sand beneath his feet, the wind buffeting his face, before he hit the water's edge. He lay prone on his board, the icy chill of Bell's Beach washing over him as the lure of the waves took hold. He'd never felt so alive. When he was in the ocean he came home.

The ocean was reliable and constant—two things he valued. Two things his parents didn't credit him as being.

He paddled harder, wishing he could leave the demons of his past behind, knowing he should confront them over the next few days.

He'd made amends with his brothers four years ago, at a time when Tom had needed his support. His relationship with his mum had thawed too, considering he didn't blame her for what happened; she'd do anything for Frank.

But things were still rough with his dad. He'd wanted to make peace many times but a healthy dose of pride, an enforced physical distance and the passing of time had put paid to that fantasy.

He'd tried making small efforts to broach the distance between them, but the residual awkwardness lingered, reinforcing his choice to stay away.

Maybe, if he was lucky, this visit home would be different.

Callie went into overdrive as an Argentinian tango blared from her surround sound.

She bounced around her lounge room, swivelling her hips and striding across the floor with arm extended and head tilted, a fake rose between her teeth.

She'd cleaned her apartment for the last two hours, increasing the volume of the music as her scrubbing, polishing and vacuuming frenzy did little to obliterate what she'd confront this afternoon.

A face-to-face meeting with her number one client.

The client her beloved CJU Designs couldn't afford to lose.

The client who might well fire her lying butt when he discovered her identity.

Archer Flett didn't do commitment. He'd made that perfectly clear in Capri eight years ago. So how would he feel when he learned he'd committed his new mega campaign to a woman he'd deliberately walked away from because they'd been getting too close.

She stubbed her toe on a wrought-iron table and swore, kicking the ornate leg again for good measure.

She was furious with herself for not confronting this issue sooner. What had she expected? Never to cross paths with Archer physically again?

Yep, that was exactly what she'd expected.

It had been three years since she'd tendered for the lucrative Torquay Tan account, completely unaware the company was owned and run by the surf world's golden boy.

It had come as a double surprise discovering the laid-back charmer she'd met eight years ago had the business nous to own a mega corporation, let alone run it. It looked as if the guy she'd once been foolish enough to fall for was full of surprises.

Now she had a chance to take on her biggest account yet: the launch of Archer's surf school in Torquay, his home town. To do it she had to meet with the man himself.

She should have bowed out gracefully, been content to be his online marketing manager for lesser accounts.

But she needed the money. Desperately.

Her mum depended on her.

The music swelled, filling her head with memories and her heart with longing. She loved the passion of Latin American music—the distinct rhythms, the sultry songs.

They reminded her of a time gone by. A time when she'd danced all night with the stars overhead and the sand under her feet. A time when she'd existed on rich pasta and cheap Chianti and whispered words of her first love.

Archer.

The music faded, along with the sentimental rubbish infiltrating her long-established common sense.

These days she didn't waste time reminiscing. She'd given up on great loves and foolish dreams.

Watching her mum go through hell had seen to that.

She was like her hot-blooded Italian father, apparently: they shared starry-eyed optimism, their impulsiveness, their passion for food and fashion and flirting. She'd considered those admirable qualities until she'd witnessed first-hand what happened when impulsive passions turned sour—her dad's selfishness knew no bounds.

And just like that she'd given up on being like her dad. She didn't give in to grand passion or fall foolhardily in love. Not any more.

Sure, she dated. She liked it. Just not enough to let anyone get too close.

As close as Archer had once been.

'Damn Archer Flett,' she muttered, kicking the table a third time for good measure.

Housework might not have worked off steam but she'd do the next best thing to prepare for this meeting.

Choose a killer business suit, blow-dry her hair and apply immaculate make-up.

Time to show Mr Hot Surfer Dude he didn't affect her after all these years.

Not much anyway.

The tiny hole-in-the-wall office of CJU Designs didn't surprise Archer. Tech geeks didn't need much space.

What did surprise him were the profuse splashes of colour adorning the walls. Slashes of magenta and crimson and turquoise against white block canvases drew his eye and brightened an otherwise nondescript space.

Small glass-topped desk, ergonomic chair, hardbacked wooden guest chair opposite. Exceedingly dull—except for that startling colour.

Almost as if the computer geek was trying to break out of a mould, trying to prove something to herself and her clients.

Well, all CJ had to prove to him was that she could handle the mega-launch he had planned for his pet project and she could hang the moon on her wall for all he cared.

He glanced around for a picture. Not for the first time he was curious about his online marketing manager.

He'd internet-searched CJU Designs extensively before hiring their services and had come up with nothing but positive PR and high praise from clients, including many sportspeople.

So he'd hired CJ, beyond impressed with her work. Crisp, clear, punctual, she always delivered on time, creating the perfect slogans, pitches and launches for any product he'd put his name to.

Trailing a finger along the dust-free desk, he wondered how she'd cope with a campaign of this size. Launching the first Flett Surf School for teens had to succeed. It was a prototype for what he planned in the surf hotspots around the world.

He'd seen too many kids in trouble—kids who hung around the beaches drinking, smoking dope, catching the occasional wave. They were aimless, trying to look cool, when in fact he'd seen the lost look in their eyes.

This was his chance to make a difference. And hopefully prove to his family just how wrong they'd been to misjudge him.

He'd never understood it—had done a lot of soul-searching to come up with one valid reason why they hadn't trusted him enough.

Had he been too blasé? Too carefree? Too narcissistic? Too wrapped up in his career to pick up the signs there'd been a major problem?

Tom and Trav hadn't helped when they'd discussed it a few years ago. He'd asked, and they'd hedged, reiterating that they'd been sworn to secrecy by Frank, embarrassed that their complicity had contributed to the ongoing gap between them.

So Archer had made a decision right then to forget his damn pride and re-bond with his brothers. They might not be the best mates they'd once been but their sometimes tense relationship now was a far improvement on the one they'd had previously—the one he still had with his dad.

It irked, not knowing the reason why they'd done it, and

their lack of trust had left a lasting legacy. One he hoped opening the surf school would go some way to rectifying.

Thinking about his family made him pace the shoebox office. He hated confined spaces. Give him the ocean expanses any day. He never felt as free as he did catching a wave, paddling out to sea, with nothing between him and the ocean but an aerodynamic sliver of fibreglass.

Nothing beat the rush.

He heard the determined click-clack of high heels striding towards the office and turned in time to see Calista Umberto enter.

His stomach went into free fall, as it had the first time he'd caught a thirty-foot wave. That rush? Seeing Callie again after all these years topped it.

While he stared like a starstruck fool, she didn't blink. In fact she didn't seem at all surprised, which could only mean one thing.

She'd been expecting him.

In that second it clicked.

CJU Designs.

Calista Jane Umberto.

The fact he remembered her middle name annoyed him as much as discovering the online marketing whiz he'd been depending on for the last three years was the woman he'd once almost lost his mind over.

His Callie.

'I'll be damned,' he muttered, crossing the small space in three strides, bundling her into his arms in an impulsive hug before he could process the fact that she'd actually taken a step back at his approach.

The frangipani fragrance hit him first—her signature bodywash that instantly resurrected memories of midnight strolls on a moonlit Capri beach, long, languorous kisses in the shade of a lemon tree, exploring every inch of the deliciously smooth skin drenched in that tempting floral scent.

Any time he'd hit an island hotspot to surf—Bali, Hawaii, Fiji—frangipanis would transport him back in time. To a time he remembered fondly, but a time fraught with danger, when he'd been captivated by a woman to the point of losing sight of the end game.

In the few seconds when her fragrance slammed his senses, he registered her rigid posture, her reluctance to be embraced.

Silently cursing himself, he released her and stepped back, searching her face for some sign that she remembered what they'd once shared.

Her lush mouth—with a ripe red gloss—flat-lined, but she couldn't hide the spark in her eyes.

Flecks of gold in a rich, deep chocolate. Eyes he'd seen glazed with passion, sparkling with enthusiasm, lighting with love.

It was the latter that had sent him running from Capri without looking back. He'd do well to remember that before indulging in a spin down memory lane and potentially ostracising his marketing manager.

'Good to see you, Archer,' she said, her tone polite and frigid and so at odds with the Callie he remembered that he almost took a step back. 'Take a seat and we'll get started.'

He shook his head, the fog of confusion increasing as he stared at this virtual stranger acting as if they barely knew each other.

He'd seen her naked, for goodness' sake. For a week straight. A long, hot, decadent week that had blown his mind in every way.

'You're not serious?'

Her stoic business persona faltered and she toyed with

the bracelet on her right wrist, turning it round and around in a gesture he'd seen often that first night in Capri.

The night they'd met. The night they'd talked for hours, strolled for ages, before ending up at his villa. The night they'd connected on so many levels he'd been terrified and yet powerless to resist her allure.

She'd been brash and brazen and beautiful, quick to laugh and parry his quips, slow to savour every twirl of linguini and rich Napolitano sauce.

She'd had a passion for everything from fresh crusty bread dipped in olive oil to hiking along pebbly beach trails to nights spent exploring each other's bodies in erotic detail.

That passionate woman he remembered was nothing like this cool, imperturbable automaton.

Except for that tell with the bracelet he would have thought she didn't remember, let alone want to acknowledge the past.

'I'm serious about getting down to business.'

The bracelet-twirling picked up pace, a giveaway that she was more rattled than she let on.

'Plenty of time for that.' He gestured towards her slimline laptop, the only thing on her desk. 'What I want to know is why you've been hiding behind your PC all this time?'

Another hit. Her eyes widened and her tongue darted out to the corner of her mouth.

A mouth designed for culinary riches and sin.

A mouth thinned in an unimpressed line so far removed from the smiles he remembered that he almost reached out with his fingertip to tilt the corners up.

'I'm not hiding behind anything,' she said, her tone as prim as her fitted black suit.

Actually, the suit wasn't all bad. Hugging all the right

curves, flaring at the cuffs and hem, ending above her knee. Combined with an emerald silk shirt hinting at cleavage, it was better than okay.

He was just grouchy because she wasn't rapt to see him. But then again, considering the way they'd parted…

'You didn't think I might like to know that the marketing whiz I e-mail regularly is someone I…'

What? Once had memorable sex with? Once knew intimately? Once might have given up his freedom for, in another time, another place? If he hadn't still been reeling from his parents' revelations?

Her eyes narrowed. 'Someone you what?'

He should have known she wouldn't let him off lightly. She hadn't back then either, when he'd told her he was skipping out.

'Someone I know,' he finished lamely, trying his signature charming grin for good measure.

Her lips merely compressed further as she swivelled away and strode to her desk. Not so bad, considering he got the opportunity to watch expensive linen shift over that memorable butt.

Damn, he loved her curves. He'd seen his fair share of bikini babes over the years—an occupational hazard and one he appreciated—but the way Callie had filled out a swimsuit?

Unforgettable.

She sat behind her desk, glaring at him as if she could read his mind. She waved at the chair opposite and he sat, thrown by her reaction. Acting professional was one thing. The ice princess act she had going on was losing appeal fast.

'Our fling wasn't relevant to our business dealings so I didn't say anything—particularly after how things ended.'

She eyeballed him, daring him to disagree. Wisely, he kept mute, interested to see where she was going with this.

'I tendered for your account without knowing you were behind the company.'

Her next sign of anything less than cool poise was when she absentmindedly tapped the space bar on her laptop with a thumb.

'When we started corresponding and worked well together, I didn't want to complicate matters.'

'Complicate them how?'

A faint pink stained her cheeks. Oh, yeah, this was starting to get real interesting.

'What do you want me to say? Any shared past tends to complicate things.'

'Only if you let it.' He hooked his hands behind his head, enjoying the battle gleam in her eyes. At last the fiery woman he knew was coming out to fight. 'Don't know about you, but I don't let *anything* interfere with my career.'

'Like I didn't know that,' she muttered, and he had the grace to acknowledge a twinge of regret.

He'd used his burgeoning surfing career to end it in Capri. It had seemed as good as excuse as any. He might as well live down to the reputation his family had tarred him with. Anything was better than telling her the truth.

'Is this going to be a problem for you?'

He threw it out there, half expecting her to say yes, hoping she'd say no.

He wasn't disappointed to see her—far from it. And the fact they'd have to spend time together in Torquay to get the marketing campaign for the surf school off the ground was a massive bonus.

Torquay... Wedding...

It was like a wave crashing over him. He floated the solution to another problem.

They'd have to spend time in Torquay for business.

He had to spend time with his overzealous family at Trav's wedding.

He had to find a date.

A bona fide city girl who'd act as a buffer between him and his family.

Lucky for him, he was looking straight at her.

Not that he'd let her know yet. He needed her expertise for this account, and by her less than welcoming reaction he'd be hard-pressed getting her to Torquay in the first place without scaring her away completely.

Yeah, he'd keep that little gem for later.

Her brows furrowed. 'What's with the smug grin?'

He leaned forward and nudged the laptop between them out of the way. 'You want this latest account?'

She nodded, a flicker of something bordering on fear in her eyes. It might make him callous, but he could work with fear. Fear meant she was probably scared of losing his lucrative business. Fear meant she might agree to accompany him to Torquay even if she had been giving him the ice treatment ever since she'd set foot in the office.

'You know this campaign will mean spending loads of one-on-one time together on the school site down at Torquay?'

Her clenched jaw made him want to laugh out loud. 'Why? I've always worked solo before. and as you can attest the results have been great.'

If she expected him to back down, she'd better think again. He'd get her to accompany him to Torquay by any means necessary—including using the campaign as blackmail.

Feigning disappointment, he shook his head. 'Sorry, a remote marketing manager won't cut it this time. I'll need you to shadow me to get a feel for the vibe I'm trying to capture with the school. The kids won't go for it otherwise.'

Her steely glare could have sliced him in two. 'For how long?'

'One week.'

She sucked in a breath, her nose wrinkling in distaste, and he bit back a laugh.

'From your previous work I'm sure you want to do this campaign justice and that's what it's going to take. You can be home in time to celebrate Christmas Day.'

Appealing to her professional pride was a master touch. She couldn't say no.

'Fine. I'll do it,' she muttered, her teeth clenching so hard he was surprised he didn't hear a crack.

'There's just one more thing.' Unable to resist teasing her, he twisted a sleek strand of silky brown hair around his finger. 'We'll be cohabiting.'

CHAPTER TWO

CALLIE stared at Archer in disbelief.

The cocky charmer was blackmailing her.

As if she'd let him get away with that.

She folded her arms, sat back, and pinned him with a disbelieving glare. 'Never thought I'd see the day hotshot Archer Flett resorted to blackmail to get a woman to shack up with him.'

His eyes sparked with admiration and she stiffened. She didn't want to remember how he'd looked at her in a similar way during their week in Capri, his expression indulgent, bordering on doting.

As if. He'd bolted all the same, admiration or not, and she'd do well to remember it.

For, as much as she'd like to tell him where he could stick his business contract, she needed the money.

'Blackmail sounds rather harsh.' He braced his forearms on her desk and leaned forward, immediately shrinking the space between them and making her breath catch. 'A bit of gentle persuasion sounds much more civilised.'

That voice… It could coax Virgins Anonymous into revoking their membership. Deep, masculine, with a hint of gravel undertone—enough to give Sean Connery healthy competition.

There was nothing gentle about Archer's persuasion.

If he decided to turn on the full arsenal of his charm she didn't stand a chance, even after all this time.

That irked the most. Eight long years during which she'd deliberately eradicated his memory, had moved on, had dealt with her feelings for him to the extent where she could handle his online marketing without flinching every time she saw his picture or received an e-mail.

Gone in an instant—wiped just like that. Courtesy of his bedroom voice, his loaded stare and irresistible charm.

'Besides, living together for the week is logical. My house has plenty of room and we'll be working on the campaign 24/7. It's sound business sense.'

Damn him. He was right.

She could achieve a lot more in seven days without factoring in travel time—especially when she had no clue where his house was or its vicinity to Torquay.

However, acknowledging that his stipulation made sense and liking it were worlds apart.

'You know I'm not comfortable with this, right?'

'Really? I hadn't picked up on that.'

He tried his best disarming grin and she deliberately glanced away. Living with him for the week might be logical for business, but having to deal with his natural charm around the clock was not good.

'Anything I can do to sweeten the deal?'

Great—he was laying the charm on thick. Her gaze snapped to his in time to catch his damnably sexy mouth curving at the corners. Her lips tingled in remembrance of how he'd smile against her mouth when he had her weak and whimpering from his kisses.

Furious at her imploding resistance, she eyeballed him with the glare that had intimidated the manager at her mum's special accommodation into giving her another extension on payment.

'Yeah, there is something you can do to sweeten the deal.' She stabbed at an envelope with a fingertip and slid it across the desk towards him. 'Sign off on my new rates. Your PA hasn't responded to my last two e-mails and I need to get paid.'

His smile faded as he took the envelope. 'You're having financial problems?'

If he only knew.

'No. I just like to have my accounts done monthly, and you've always been prompt in the past...'

Blessedly prompt. The Torquay Tan account had single-handedly launched her business into the stratosphere and kept it afloat. If she ever lost it...

In that moment the seriousness of the situation hit her. She shouldn't be antagonising Archer. She should be jumping through whatever hoop he presented her with—adding a somersault and a *ta-da* flourish for good measure.

She had to secure this new campaign. CJU Designs would skyrocket in popularity, and her mum would continue to be cared for.

She had no other option but to agree.

'Just so we're clear. If I accompany you to Torquay, the surf school campaign is mine?'

His mocking half salute did little to calm the nerves twisting her belly into pretzels.

'All yours, Cal.'

She didn't know what unnerved her more. The intimate way the nickname he'd given her dripped off his tongue or the way his eyes sparked with something akin to desire.

She should be ecstatic that she'd secured the biggest campaign of her career.

Instead, as her pulse ramped up to keep pace with her flipping heart, all she could think was *at what price*?

* * *

Archer didn't like gloating. He'd seen enough of it on the surf circuit—arrogant guys who couldn't wait to glory over their latest win.

But the second Callie's agreement to accompany him to Torquay fell from her lush lips he wanted to strut around the office with his fists pumping in a victory salute.

An over-the-top reaction? Maybe. But having Callie by his side throughout the Christmas Eve wedding festivities—even if she didn't know it yet—would make the event and its guaranteed emotional ra-ra bearable.

He'd suffered through enough Torquay weddings to know the drill by now. Massive marquees, countless kisses from extended rellies he didn't know, back-slapping and one-upmanship from old mates, and the inevitable match-making between him and every single female under thirty in the whole district.

His mum hated the dates he brought home each year, and tried to circumvent him with less-than-subtle fix-ups: notoriously predictable, sweet, shy local girls she hoped would tempt him to settle down in Torquay and produce a brood of rowdy rug-rats.

It was the same every wedding. The same every year, for that matter, when he returned home for his annual visit. A visit primarily made out of obligation rather than any burning desire to be constantly held up as the odd one out in the Flett family.

It wasn't intentional, for his folks and his brothers tried to carry on as if nothing had happened, but while he'd for-given them for shutting him out in the past the resultant awkwardness still lingered.

He'd steadily withdrawn, stayed away because of it, pre-ferring to be free. Free to go where he wanted, when he wanted. Free from emotional attachments that invariably let him down. Free to date fun-loving, no strings attached women who didn't expect much beyond dinner and drinks rather than an engagement and a bassinet.

His gaze zeroed in on Callie as she fielded an enquiry on the phone, her pen scrawling at a frenetic pace as she jotted notes, the tip of her tongue protruding between her lips.

Callie had been that girl once. The kind of girl who wanted the picket fence dream, the equivalent of his ultimate nightmare. Did she still want that?

The finger on her left hand remained ringless, he saw as he belatedly realised he should have checked if she was seeing anyone before coercing her into heading down to Torquay on the pretext of business when in fact she'd be his date for the wedding.

Then again, she'd agreed, so his assumption that she was currently single was probably safe.

Not that she'd fallen in with his plan quickly. She'd made him work for it, made him sweat. And he had a feeling her capitulation had more to do with personal reasons than any great desire to make this campaign the best ever.

That flicker of fear when she'd thought he might walk and take his business with him… Not that he would have done it. Regardless of whether she'd wanted to come or not CJU would have had the surf school campaign in the bag. She'd proved her marketing worth many times over the last few years, and while he might be laid back on the circuit he was tough in his business.

Success meant security. Ultimately success meant he was totally self-sufficient and didn't have to depend on anyone, for he'd learned the hard way that depending on people, even those closest to you, could end in disappointment and sadness and pain.

It was what drove him every day, that quest for independence, not depending on anyone, even family, for anything.

After his folks' betrayal it was what had driven him away from Callie.

He chose to ignore his insidious voice of reason. The last thing he needed was to get sentimental over memories.

She hung up the phone, her eyes narrowing as she caught sight of him lounging in the doorway. 'You still here?'

'We're not finished.'

He only just caught her muttered, 'Could've fooled me.'

As much as it pained him to revisit the past, he knew he'd have to bring it up in order to get past her obvious snit.

He did not want a date glaring daggers at him all night; his mum would take it as a sure-fire sign to set one of her gals onto him.

'Do we need to clear the air?'

She arched an eyebrow in an imperious taunt. 'I don't know. Do we?'

Disappointed, he shook his head. 'You didn't play games. One of the many things I admired about you.'

Her withering glare wavered and dipped, before pinning him with renewed accusation. 'We had a fling in the past. Yonks ago. I'm over it. You're over it. There's no air to clear. Ancient history. The next week is business, nothing more.'

'Then why are you so antagonistic?'

She opened her mouth to respond, then snapped it shut, her icy façade faltering as she ran a hand through her hair in another uncertain tell he remembered well.

She'd done it when they'd first met at a beachside vendor's, when they'd both reached for the last chilled lemonade at the same time. She'd done it during their first dinner at a tiny trattoria tucked into an alley. And she'd done it when he'd taken her back to his hotel for the first time.

In every instance he'd banished her uncertainty with

practised charm, but after the way they'd parted he doubted it would work in this instance.

'Cal—'

'Us being involved in the past complicates this campaign and I'm not a huge fan of complications.'

She blurted it without meeting his eye, her gaze fixed on her laptop screen.

He wished she'd look at him so he could see how deeply this irked, or if she was trying to weasel out of the deal.

'You said it yourself. It's in the past. So why should it complicate anything?' He didn't want to push her, but her antagonism left him no choice. 'Unless...'

'What?' Her head snapped up, her wary gaze locking on his, and in that instant he had his answer before he asked the question.

The spark they'd once shared was there, flickering in the depths of rich brown, deliberately cloaked in evasive shadows.

'Unless you still feel something?'

'I'm many things. A masochist isn't one of them.'

She stood so quickly her chair slid backward on its castors and slammed into the wall. The noise didn't deter her as she stalked towards him, defiant in high heels.

With her eyes flashing warning signals he chose to ignore, he stepped back into the office, meeting her halfway.

Before he could speak she held up her hand. 'I'm not a fool, Archer. We were attracted in Capri, we're both single, and we're going to be spending time together on this campaign. Stands to reason a few residual sparks may fly.' Her hand snagged in her hair again and she almost wrenched it out in exasperation. 'It won't mean anything. I have a job to do, and there's no way I'll jeopardise that by making another mistake.'

He reached for her before he could second-guess, gripping her upper arms, giving her no room to move. 'We weren't a mistake.'

'Yeah? Then why did you run?'

He couldn't respond—not without telling her the truth. And that wasn't an option.

So he did the next best thing.

He released her, turned his back, and walked away.

'And you're still running,' she murmured.

Her barb registered, and served to make him stride away that little bit faster.

CHAPTER THREE

CALLIE strode towards Johnston Street and her favourite Spanish bar.

Some girls headed home to a chick-flick and tub of ice-cream when they needed comfort. She headed for Rivera's.

'Hola, querida.' Arturo Rivera blew her a kiss from behind the bar and she smiled in return, some of her tension instantly easing.

Artie knew about her situation: the necessity for her business to thrive in order to buy the best care for her mum. He knew her fears, her insecurities. He'd been there from the start, this reserved gentleman in a porkpie hat who'd lost his wife to the disease that would eventually claim her mum.

She hadn't wanted to attend a support group, but her mum's doc had insisted it would help in the disease's management and ultimately help her mum.

So she'd gone along, increasingly frustrated and helpless and angry, so damn angry, that her vibrant, fun-loving mother had been diagnosed with motor neurone disease.

She'd known nothing about her mum's symptoms until it had been too late. Nora had hidden them well: the stumbling due to weakness in her leg muscles, her difficulty holding objects due to weak hands, her swallowing difficulties and the occasional speech slur.

The first Callie had learned of it was when her mum had invited her to accompany her to see a neurologist. Nora hated needles, and apparently having an electromyograph, where they stuck needles in her muscles to measure electrical activity, was worse to bear than the actual symptoms.

The diagnosis had floored them both—especially the lack of a cure and mortality rates. Though in typical determined Nora fashion her mum had continued living independently until her symptoms had made it impossible to do so.

Nora had refused to be a burden on her only daughter, so Callie had found the best care facility around—one with top neurologists, speech, occupational and physiotherapists, psychologists, nurses and palliative care, while trying not to acknowledge her mum's steady deterioration.

It was as if she could *see* the nerve cells failing, resulting in the progressive muscle weakness that would eventually kill her mum.

So she focussed on the good news: Nora's sight, smell, taste, sensation, intellect and memory wouldn't be affected. Nora would always know her, even at the end, and that thought sustained her through many a crying jag late at night, when the pain of impending loss crowded in and strangled her forced bravery.

To compound her stress she'd had to reluctantly face the fact she had a fifty-fifty chance of inheriting it too. She hadn't breathed all through the genetic testing consultation, when the doctors had explained that Nora's motor neurone disease was caused by mutations in the SOD1 gene. That tiny superoxide dismutase one gene, located on chromosome twenty-one, controlled her fate.

Insomnia had plagued her in the lead-up to her testing, and the doctor's clinical facts had been terrifying as they echoed through her head: people with the faulty gene had a high chance of developing MND in later life, or could develop symptoms in their twenties.

Like her.

She'd worried herself sick for days after the test, and even though it had come back clear—she didn't carry the mutated gene—she'd never fully shaken the feeling that she had a swinging axe grazing the back of her neck, despite the doc's convincing argument that many people *with* the faulty gene didn't go on to develop MND.

Then the worry had given way to guilt. Guilt that she was the lucky one in her family.

During this time the support group had been invaluable. Artie had been there, just as frustrated, just as angry. He'd lost his wife of forty years.

They'd bonded over espresso and biscotti, gradually revealing their bone-deep resentment and helpless fury at a disease that had no cure. Those weekly meetings had led to an invitation to Rivera's, a place that had instantly become home.

She loved the worn, pockmarked wooden floor, the rich mahogany bar that ran the breadth of the back wall, the maroon velvet embossed wallpaper that created a cosy ambience beckoning patrons to linger over delicious tapas and decadent sangria.

This was where she'd started to thaw, where the deliberate numbness enclosing her aching heart at the injustice of what her mum faced had melted.

This was where she'd come to eat, to chat and to dance.

She lived for the nights when Artie cleared the tables and chairs, cranked up the music, and taught Spanish dances to anyone eager to learn.

Those nights were the best—when she could forget how her life had changed that momentous day when she'd learned of her mum's diagnosis.

She nodded at familiar faces as she weaved through tables towards the bar, her heart lightening with every step as Artie waved his hands in the air, gesturing at her usual spot.

'You hungry, *querida*?'

Considering the knot of nerves in her stomach, the last thing she felt like doing was eating, but if she didn't Artie would know something was wrong.

And she didn't feel like talking about the cause of her angst. Not when she'd spent the fifteen-minute walk to the bar trying to obliterate Archer from her mind.

'Maybe the daily special?'

Artie winked. 'Coming right up.'

As he spooned marinated octopus, garlic olives, *banderillas*, *calamares fritos* and *huevos relleños de gambas* onto a terracotta platter, she mentally rummaged for a safe topic of conversation—one that wouldn't involve blurting about the blackmailing guy who had once stolen her heart.

He slid the plate in front of her, along with her usual espresso. 'So, are you going to tell me what's wrong before your coffee or after?'

She opened her mouth to brush off his astute observation, but one glance at the shrewd gleam in his eyes stalled her. She knew that look. The look of a father figure who wouldn't quit till he'd dragged the truth out of her.

'It's nothing, really—'

He tut-tutted. '*Querida*, I've known you for more than seven years.' He pointed to his bald pate and wrinkled forehead. 'These may indicate the passage of time, but up here...?' He tapped his temple. 'As sharp as Banderas's sword in *Zorro*.'

She chuckled. If Artie had his way Antonio Banderas would be Spain's president.

He folded his arms and rested them on the bar. 'You know I'm going to stay here until you tell me.'

'What about your customers?'

'That's what I pay the staff for.' He grinned. 'Now, are you going to tell, or do I have to ply you with my finest sangria?'

She held up her hands. 'I'm starting work early tomorrow, so no sangria.'

How tempting it sounded. What she wouldn't give to down a jug of Artie's finest, get blotto, and forget the fact she had to accompany Archer to Torquay tomorrow.

'Fine.' She pushed a few olives around her plate before laying down her fork. 'CJU Designs scored its biggest account ever today.'

Artie straightened and did a funny flamenco pirouette. 'That's brilliant. Well done, *querida*.'

'Yeah, it'll take care of mum's bills for the next year at least, thank goodness.'

Artie's exuberance faded. 'How is Nora?'

'The same. Happy, determined, putting on a brave face.'

Something *she* was finding increasingly hard to do when she visited and saw the signs that her mum's condition was worsening. While Nora coped with her wheelchair, relaxed as if she was lounging in her favourite recliner, Callie watched for hand tremors or lapses in speech or drifting off.

She couldn't relax around her mum any more. The effort of hiding her sadness clamped her throat in a stranglehold, taking its toll. She grew more exhausted after every visit, and while she never for one second regretted spending as much time as possible with her mum, she hated the inevitability of this horrid disease.

Artie patted her hand. 'Give her my best next time you see her.'

'Shall do.'

That was another thing that bugged her about this Torquay trip. She'd have to give all her attention to the account in the early set-up—and to the account's aggravating owner—which meant missing out on seeing her mum for the week before Christmas or long drives to and from the beachside town. Which would lead to Archer poking his nose into her business, asking why she had to visit her mum so often, and she didn't want to divulge her private life to him.

Not now, when things were strictly business.

'If this account has alleviated some of your financial worries, why do you look like this?' Artie's exaggerated frown made her smile.

'Because simple solutions often mask convoluted complications.'

'Cryptic.'

'Not really.' She huffed out a long breath. 'The owner of the company behind this new account is an old friend.'

'Ah...so that's it.'

She didn't like the crafty glint in Artie's eyes much—his knowing smile less.

'This...friend...is he a past *amor*?'

Had she loved Archer? After the awful break-up, and in the following months when she'd returned to Melbourne and preferred reading to dating, she'd wondered if the hollowness in her heart, the constant gripe in her belly and the annoying wanderlust to jump back on a plane and follow him around the world's surfing hotspots was love.

She'd almost done it once, after seeing a snippet of him at the Pipeline in Hawaii three months after she'd returned from Europe. She'd gone as far as logging on, choosing flights, but when it had come to paying the arrow had hovered over 'confirm' for an agonising minute before the memory of their parting had resurfaced and she'd shut the whole thing down.

That moment had been her wake-up call, and she'd deliberately worked like a maniac so she could fall into bed at the end of a day exhausted and hopefully dream-free.

Her mum had been diagnosed four weeks later, and as a distraction from Archer it had been a doozy.

Now here he was, strutting into her life, as confident and charming and gorgeous as ever. And as dangerously seductive as all those years ago. For, no matter how many times she rationalised that their week together would be strictly business, the fact remained that they'd once shared a helluva spark. She'd better pack her fire extinguisher just in case.

Artie held up his hands. 'You don't have to answer. I can see your feelings for this old *amor* written all over your face.'

'I don't love him.'

Artie merely smiled and moved down the bar towards an edgy customer brandishing an empty sangria jug, leaving her to ponder the conviction behind her words.

While Callie would have loved to linger over a sangria or two when the Spanish Flamenco band fired up, she had more important things to do.

Like visiting her mum.

Nora hated it when she fussed, so these days she kept her visits to twice weekly—an arrangement they were both happy with.

The doctors had given her three years. The doctors didn't know what a fighter Nora Umberto was. She'd lasted seven, and while her tremors seemed to increase every time Callie visited the spark of determination in her mum's eyes hadn't waned.

After the life she'd led, no way would Nora go out without a bang. She continued to read to the other residents and direct the kitchen hands to prepare exotic dishes—dishes she'd tried first-hand during her travels around the world, during which she'd met Bruno Umberto.

Callie's dad might not have stuck around long in his first marriage—or any of his subsequent three marriages, for that matter—but thankfully Nora's love of cosmopolitan cuisine had stuck. Callie had grown up on fajitas, ratatouille, korma and Szechuan—a melting pot of tastes to accompany her mum's adventurous stories.

She'd never really known her dad, but Nora had been enough parent and then some. Dedicated to raising her daughter, Nora hadn't dated until after she'd graduated high school and moved out. Even then her relationships had lasted only a scant few months. Callie had always wondered if her mum's exuberance had been too much for middle-aged guys who'd expected Martha Stewart and ended up with Lara Croft.

As she entered the shaded forecourt of Colldon Special Accommodation Home she knew that made it all the harder to accept—the fact her go-get-'em mother had been cut down in her prime by a devastating illness no amount of fighting could conquer.

She signed in, slipped a visitor's lanyard over her neck and headed towards the rear of the sandstone building. As she strolled down the pastel-carpeted corridor she let the peace of the place infuse her: the piped rainforest sounds, the subtle scent of lemon and ginger essential oils being diffused from air vents, the colours on the walls transitioning from muted mauve to sunny daffodil.

Colldon felt more like an upmarket boutique hotel than a special home and Callie would do whatever it took to ensure her mum remained here.

Including shacking up with Archer Flett for a week to work on his precious campaign.

She shook her head, hoping that would dispel the image of her agreeing to his demands. It didn't, and all she could see was his startling aquamarine eyes lighting with a fire she remembered all too well when she'd said yes.

She'd been a fool thinking she had the upper hand: she'd known his identity; he hadn't known the woman behind CJU Designs. However, the element of surprise meant little when he'd been the one who ended up ousting her from her smug comfort zone.

Her neck muscle spasmed and she rubbed it as she entered Nora's room. She didn't knock. No one knocked. Her mum's door was perpetually open to whoever wanted to pop in for a chat.

Vibrant, sassy, alive: three words that summed up Nora Umberto.

But as she caught sight of her mum struggling to zip up her cardigan that last word taunted her.

Alive. For how much longer?

She swallowed the lump of sadness welling in her throat, pasted a smile on her face and strode into the room.

'Hey, Mum, how you doing?'

Nora's brilliant blue eyes narrowed as she gestured at the zip with a shaky hand. 'Great—until some bright spark dressed me in this today.'

Her defiant smile made Callie's heart ache.

'Buttons are a pain, but these plastic zips aren't a whole lot better.'

Need a hand? The words hovered on Callie's lips but she clamped them shut. Nora didn't like being treated like an invalid. She liked accepting help less.

Instead, Callie perched on the armchair opposite and ignored the increasing signs that her mum was struggling.

'I'll be away next week.'

Nora instantly perked up. If Callie had to sit through one more lecture about all work and no play she'd go nuts. Not that she could blame her mum. Nora loved hearing stories of Rivera's and dancing and going out, living vicariously through her.

Callie embellished those tales, making her life sound more glamorous than it was. Her mum had enough to worry about without concern for a daughter who dated only occasionally, went Spanish dancing twice a week, and did little else but work. Work that paid the hefty Colldon bills.

'Holiday?'

Callie shook her head. 'Work. In Torquay.'

She said it casually, as if heading to the beachside town *didn't* evoke visions of sun, surf and sexy guys in wetsuits.

Particularly one sexy guy. Who she'd been lucky enough to see without a wetsuit many years ago on another sun-drenched beach.

'You sure it's work?'

Nora leaned so far forward in her wheelchair she almost toppled forward, and Callie had to fold her arms to stop from reaching out.

'You've got a glow.'

'It's an "I'm frazzled to be going away the week before Christmas" glow.'

Nora sagged, her cheekiness instantly dimming. 'You'll be away for Christmas?'

Callie leaned forward and squeezed her mum's hand, careful not to scratch the tissue-thin skin. 'I'll be back in time for Christmas lunch. You think I'd miss Colldon's cranberry stuffing?'

Nora chuckled. 'You know, I wouldn't mind if you missed Christmas with me if your trip involved a hot young man. But work? That's no excuse.'

Ironic. Her trip involved a hot young man *and* work, and she had a feeling she'd need to escape both after a long week in Torquay.

She stood and bent to kiss her mum's cheek. 'Sorry it's a flying visit, but I need to go home and pack. I'm leaving first thing in the morning.'

To her surprise, Nora snagged her hand as she straightened, holding on with what little strength she had.

'Don't forget to have a little fun amid all that work, Calista.' She squeezed—the barest of pressure. 'You know life's too short.'

Blinking back the sudden sting of tears, Callie nodded. 'Sure thing, Mum. And ring me if you need anything.'

Nora released her hand, managing a feeble wave. 'I'll be fine. Go work, play, have fun.'

Callie intended to work. As for the fun and play, she didn't dare associate those concepts with Archer.

Look what had happened the last time she'd done that.

Archer didn't jerk women around, and after the way Callie had reacted to him yesterday he shouldn't push her buttons. But that was exactly what he'd done in hiring the fire-engine red Roadster for their trip to Torquay.

She'd recognise the significance of the car, but would she call him on it?

By the tiny crease between her brows and her compressed lips as she stalked towards him, he doubted it.

The carefree, teasing girl he'd once known had disappeared behind this uptight, reserved shadow of her former self. What had happened to snuff the spark out?

'Still travelling light?' He held out his hand for her overnight bag.

She flung it onto the back seat in response.

'Oo-kay, then. Guess it's going to be a long trip.'

He glimpsed a flicker of remorse as she slid onto the passenger seat, her rigid back and folded arms indicative of her absolute reluctance to be here. To be anywhere near him.

It ticked him off.

They'd once been all over each other, laughing and chatting and touching, a hand-hold here, a thigh squeeze there. When she'd smiled at him he'd felt a buzz akin to riding the biggest tube.

But you walked away anyway.

That was all he needed. For his voice of reason to give him a kick in the ass too.

But she hadn't been forthcoming during their meeting yesterday, and he'd be damned if he'd put up with her foul mood for the next week.

If he showed up at Trav's wedding with her in this snit his mum would know Callie was a fake date and be inquisitive, effectively ruining his buffer zone.

Yeah, because that was the only reason he minded her mood...

He revved the engine, glanced over his shoulder and pulled into traffic. 'You know it's ninety minutes to Torquay, right?'

'Yeah.'

Her glance barely flicked his way behind Audrey Hepburnesque sunglasses that conveniently covered half her face.

'You planning on maintaining the long face the entire way? Do I need to resort to I-spy and guess the number-plate to get a laugh?'

'I'm here to work—'

'Bull.'

He swerved into a sidestreet, earning momentary whiplash and several honks for his trouble.

'What the heck—?'

He kissed her, pouring all his frustration with her frosty behaviour into the kiss.

She resisted at first, but he wouldn't back off. He might have done this to prove a point, but once his lips touched hers he remembered—in excruciating detail—what it had been like to kiss her.

And he wanted more.

He moved his mouth across hers—light, teasing, taunting her to capitulate.

She remained tight-lipped—until his hand caressed the nape of her neck and slid into her hair, his fingertips brushing her scalp in the way he knew she liked.

She gave a little protesting groan and he sensed the moment of surrender when she placed her palm on his chest and half-heartedly pushed. Her lips softened a second later.

He didn't hesitate, taking advantage of her compliance by deepening the kiss, sweeping his tongue into her mouth to find hers, challenging her to deny them, confident she wouldn't.

For what seemed like a glorious eternity they made out like a besotted couple. Then he eased his hand out of her hair, his lips lingering on hers for a bittersweet second before he sat back.

What he saw shocked him more than the rare times he'd been ragdolled by a gnarly wave.

The old Callie was back.

Her brown eyes sparkled, her lush mouth curved smugly at the corners and she *glowed*.

Hell, he'd wanted to get her to lighten up. He hadn't counted on the winded feeling now making his lungs seize.

Being wiped out by a killer wave was easier than this.

But in the few seconds it took him to come up with something casual to say Callie closed off. Her glow gave way to a frown and shadows effectively cloaked the sparkle.

'Happy you sneaked a kiss for old times' sake? Did you want to prove something?'

He shook his head, still befuddled by the strength of his reaction to a kiss that should have meant nothing.

'I wanted to make a mockery of your "just work" declaration.'

She quirked an elegant brow. 'And did you think one little kiss would do that?'

He hadn't. Been thinking, that was. Like feeling the overwhelming rush he got from riding the perfect set on a huge swell he'd done the spontaneous thing. And now he had to live with the consequences: working alongside Callie for the next seven days while trying to forget how incredible she looked all mussed and vulnerable, and how she tasted—like chocolate and coffee.

'I guess I'm just annoyed by your attitude and I wanted to rattle you.'

As much as it turned out she still rattled *him*.

He expected her to bristle, to retreat behind a mask of cool indifference. He didn't expect her to unravel before his eyes.

'Hell, are you *crying*?'

He reached out to hold her, but stopped when she scooted away.

She dashed a hand across her eyes before turning to stare out of the window, her profile stoic and tugging at his heartstrings.

'It's not you. I'm just juggling some other stuff, and it's taking a toll even though I have a handle on it.'

He'd never heard her sound so soft, so vulnerable, and he clamped down on the urge to haul her into his arms. Mixed messages be damned.

'Anything I can do to help?'

'Keep being a smartass. That should make me laugh.'

The quiver in her voice had him reaching across, gently cupping her chin and turning her towards him.

'I can back off if you're going through stuff. Cut the jokes. No kissing. That kind of thing.'

She managed a watery smile. 'No kissing's a given while we work together. The jokes I can handle.'

As she gnawed on her bottom lip realisation slammed into him as if he was pitching over the falls.

She probably had boyfriend troubles.

'Is it another guy? Because I can kick his ass—'

'Not a guy.'

Her smile morphed into a grin and it was like surfacing for air after being submerged underwater for too long.

She held a hand over her heart. 'I promise to lighten up. I'm just…overworked and tired and grumpy in general.'

'That seventh dwarf had nothing on you,' he mumbled, eliciting the expected chuckle—the first time he'd heard her sound remotely light-hearted since yesterday. 'Maybe you should thank me for kissing you. Because you've had an epiphany and—'

'Don't push your luck,' she said, tempering her growl with a wink, catapulting him back to Capri, where she'd winked at him in a tiny dinghy the moment before they'd entered the Blue Grotto, warning him to be careful because the cave was renowned for proposals and he might succumb.

She'd been teasing, but it had been the beginning of the end for them: no matter how carefree their fling, he'd wondered if Callie secretly harboured hopes for more.

And Archer had already learnt that the price paid for loving wasn't one he was willing to pay.

'Okay, so if kissing's off the agenda, work it is,' he said, holding her gaze for several long, loaded moments, daring her to disagree, hoping she would.

'Just work,' she echoed, before elbowing him and pointing at the road. 'If we ever get to Torquay, that is.'

As he reversed out of the sidestreet he knew he should be glad he'd cracked Callie's brittle, reserved outer shell.

But now he'd seen the woman beneath—the same warm, lush woman who'd almost snared his heart eight years ago—he wondered if he should be glad or scared.

CHAPTER FOUR

OKAY, so Callie hadn't been thinking straight since Archer had strolled into her office yesterday.

She'd been caught off guard by the gorgeous familiarity of him, by his outlandish suggestion to live with him for a week while they work, by his demand to agree or lose the account.

She'd also been worried about leaving Nora for the seven days before Christmas once she'd given in to secure the campaign—a worry that hadn't eased despite seeing her mum yesterday.

Her head had been filled with *stuff.* That was the only explanation for why she hadn't seen that kiss coming.

He'd done it out of frustration. She could see that now. He'd wanted to snap her out of her funk, to prove a point.

So what was the rationale behind her responding?

She'd assumed she could handle their cosy living arrangements for business's sake.

She hadn't counted on *this*. This slightly manic, out-of-control feeling because despite her vow to remain platonic he could undermine her with one itty-bitty kiss.

Damn.

She'd been silent for most of the trip, jotting fake notes for the campaign, needing to concentrate on something

other than her tingling lips. Thankfully he'd respected her
need for silence until about twenty miles out of Torquay.

They'd arrived, and she hadn't been able to believe her
eyes.

As he'd steered up the winding, secluded street and
pulled up outside Archer had called it his beach shack.

Massive understatement. *Huge.* Considering she now
stood in a glass-enclosed lounge room as big as her entire
apartment, with floor-to-ceiling glass and three-hundred-
and-sixty-degree views of the Tasman Sea.

This place was no shack.

The pale blue rugs on gleaming ash floorboards, the
sand-coloured suede sofas, the modern glass coffee tables—all screamed class, and were nothing like the mis-
matched furniture in the log cabin *shack* she'd imagined.

Archer had never been into material things when they'd
first met. It looked as if being a world pro five years running changed a guy.

'I put your bags in the first guest room on the right,'
he said, his bare feet barely making a sound as he padded
up behind her.

Another thing she remembered: his dislike for footwear.
It hadn't mattered much in Capri, when they'd spent many
hours on the beach, and she'd hidden a smile as he'd unlocked the door here, dumped their bags inside and slipped
off his loafers.

She liked him barefoot. He had sexy feet. They matched
the rest of him.

'Thanks.'

He wiggled his eyebrows. 'Right next to my room, in
case you were wondering.'

'I wasn't.' Her heart gave a betraying kick.

'Liar,' he said, snagging a strand of hair and winding
it around his finger, tugging gently.

She knew what he was doing—flirting to keep her smiling. But she *sooo* wasn't going to play this game. Not after that dangerous kiss in the car.

'You still feel the buzz.' His gaze strayed to her lips and she could have sworn they tingled in remembrance.

The smart thing to do would be to lie, but she'd never been any good at it. That was how they'd hooked up in the first place—because of her complete inability to deny how incredibly hot she'd found the laid-back surfer.

He'd romanced her and she'd let him, fully aware that their week in Capri was nothing more than a holiday fling. Pity her impressionable heart hadn't caught up with logic and she'd fallen for him anyway. Her feelings had made it so much harder to get over him—especially after the way he'd ended it.

She'd do well to remember their break-up, not how his kiss had zapped her synapses in the car and reawakened a host of dormant memories she'd be better off forgetting.

'As I recall, didn't we have a conversation in the car about focussing on work?'

His finger brushed her scalp as he wound the strand all the way and she suppressed a tidal wave of yearning.

'You didn't answer my question.' His finger trailed along her hairline, skirting her temple, around her ear, lingering on the soft skin beneath it and she held her breath.

He'd kissed her there many times, until she'd been mindless with wanting him.

'That kiss you sprung on me in the car? Out of line. Business as usual this week. That's it.'

'Protesting much?'

'Archer, don't—'

'Go on, admit it. We still share a spark.'

His mouth eased into a wicked grin and she held up a

hand to ward him off. 'Doesn't mean we'll be doing anything about it.'

She expected him to ask why. She expected him to undermine her rationale with charm. Instead he stopped touching her, a shadow skating across his eyes before he nodded.

'You're right; we've got a ton of work to do. Best we don't get distracted.'

'Sounds like a plan,' she said, struggling to keep the disappointment out of her voice.

But something must have alerted him to the raging indecisive battle she waged inside—flee or fling—because he added, 'But once work is out of the way who knows what we'll get up to?'

She rolled her eyes, not dignifying him with a response, and his chuckles taunted her as she headed for the sanctity of her room.

She needed space. She needed time out. She needed to remember why getting involved with a nomad charmer again was a bad idea.

Because right now she was in danger of forgetting.

After what he'd been through with his family, Archer hated dishonesty.

Which made what he was doing with Callie highly unpalatable. He needed to tell her about being his date for the wedding pronto.

They'd arrived at the house three hours ago, and she'd made herself scarce on the pretext of unpacking and doing some last-minute research.

He knew better.

That impulsive kiss in the car might have been to prove a point but somewhere along the way it had morphed into something bigger than both of them.

He'd been so damn angry at her perpetual iciness he'd wanted to shock the truth out of her: the spark was still there.

Oh, it was there all right, and interestingly his little experiment had gone awry. He'd been shocked too.

He'd asked her to accompany him here for work—and the wedding. Nothing more, nothing less.

That kiss? Major reality check.

For there was something between them—something latent and simmering, just waiting to ignite.

Hell.

Way to go with complicating matters.

Best to take a step back and simplify—starting with divulging his addendum to her week-long stay.

He knocked twice at her bedroom door. 'Lunch is ready.'

The door creaked open and she stuck her head around it. What did she think? He'd catch sight of the bed and want to ravish her on the spot?

Hmmm…good point.

'Raincheck?'

He exhaled in exasperation. 'I need my marketing manager in peak form, which means no skipping meals—no matter how distasteful you find my company.'

'It's not that.' She blushed. 'I tend to grab snatched meals whenever I remember, so I don't do a sit-down lunch very often.'

'Lucky for you we're not sitting down.' He snagged her hand, meeting the expected resistance when she pulled back. He tugged harder. 'It's no big deal, Cal. Fish and chips on the beach. You can have your head buried behind your computer again in thirty minutes.'

Her expression softened. 'Give me five minutes and I'll meet you outside.'

'Is this a ploy so I have to release your hand and you'll abscond?'

She chuckled, a welcome, happy sound after her apparent snit. 'It's a ploy to use the bathroom.' She held up her hands. 'No other ulterior motives or escape plans in the works—promise.'

'In that case I'll see you down there.' He squeezed her hand before releasing it. 'But more than five minutes and I get the best piece of fish.'

'You're on.'

Thankfully she only kept him waiting three, and he'd barely had time to spread the picnic blanket on the sand before she hit the beach running.

His breath caught as he watched her scuffing sand and snagging her hair into a loose knot at the nape of her neck. The actions were so reminiscent of their time in Capri he wanted to run half way to meet her.

Not liking how fast she'd got under his skin, he busied himself with unwrapping the paper and setting out the lemon wedges and salt sachets alongside the chips and grilled fish. Anything to keep his hands busy and resisting the urge to sweep her into his arms when she got close enough.

'That smells amazing,' she said, flopping down on the blanket next to him. 'But you said no sitting down.'

'Trivialities.' He pushed the paper towards her. 'Eat.'

And they did, making short work of the meal in companionable silence. He hadn't aimed for romance but there was a certain implied intimacy that had more to do with their shared past than any concerted effort now.

The comfortableness surprised him. Considering her reservations about heading to Torquay with him in the first place, and then her absentee act all morning, he'd expected awkwardness.

This relaxed ambience was good. All the better to spring his surprise.

'I need to ask you a favour.'

She licked the last grains of salt off her fingers—an innocuous, innocent gesture that shot straight to his groin.

'What is it?'

Now or never. 'My youngest brother Travis is getting married Christmas Eve and I'd like you to be my date.'

She stared at him in open-mouthed shock, her soda can paused halfway to her lips.

'You're asking me to be your *date*?'

She made it sound as if he'd asked her to swim naked in a sea full of ravenous sharks.

'We're not heading back 'til Christmas Day, and it doesn't make sense for you to spend Christmas Eve alone when you could come to what'll basically be a whoop-up party, so I thought you might like to come.'

'I don't have anything to wear,' she blurted, her horror-stricken expression not waning.

So much for that spark he'd imagined when they'd kissed.

'There are a couple of local boutiques, but honestly it'll be a pretty casual affair.'

'Well, you've thought of everything, haven't you?'

Her eyes narrowed, and he braced for the obvious question.

'Why didn't you ask me before we got here?'

Several lame-ass excuses sprang to mind, but he knew nothing but honesty would work now.

'Because I knew you wouldn't come.'

Her fingers clenched so hard she dented the soda can. 'So the business thing was an excuse?'

'No way. I need this surf school campaign to fly and

you're the best.' He tried an endearing grin. 'I just figured we could kill two birds with one stone.'

'I could kill *you*,' she muttered, placing her soda can on the sand and hugging her knees to her chest. 'I don't like being taken for a fool.'

'You know that's not how I see you.'

She rested her cheek on her knees, her sidelong glance oddly vulnerable. 'How do I know? It's been eight years since I've seen you.'

Hating the certainty pinging through him that he'd majorly stuffed this up, he scooted closer and draped an arm across her shoulders, surprised when she didn't shrug it off.

'Honestly? I wanted to tell you, but I was pretty thrown at your office, and you weren't exactly welcoming so I took the easy way out and focussed on the business side of things. Forgive me?'

'I'll think about it,' she said, her tone underlined by a hint of ice as the corners of her mouth were easing upwards.

'Is it that much of a hardship to be my date for an evening?'

'Considering I don't know you any more, yeah.'

'Easily rectified.'

Before he could second-guess the impulse he leaned across and kissed her.

It was nothing like his reckless prove-a-point kiss in the car. This time it just felt *right*.

She fought him initially, trying to pull away, but his hand slid around the back of her head, anchoring her, and he sensed the second she gave in.

Her lips softened and she moaned, the barest of sounds but enough for him to deepen the kiss, until the roaring in his ears matched the pounding of the surf crashing metres from their feet.

He had no idea how long the kiss lasted. A few seconds. An eternity. But when it ended he wished it hadn't.

'You've gotta stop doing that.' She shoved him away—hard.

'Sorry,' he said, not meaning it, and by her raised eyebrow she knew it.

'Hollow apologies after the fact don't cut it.' She jabbed a finger at his chest. 'And neither do those kisses. Quit it, okay?'

'Hey, I'm an impulsive guy. You can't blame me—'

'You want me to be your date for the wedding?'

'Yeah.'

'Then no more funny business.' Her gaze dropped to his lips, lingered, and he could have sworn he glimpsed longing. 'This campaign means a lot to both of us, so let's keep our minds on the job, okay?'

'Okay.'

He wanted to lighten the mood, end on a frivolous note. 'Maybe I wanted that kiss to prove it won't be so far-fetched for you to pretend to be a devoted date at the wedding—'

'You're impossible,' she said, leaping to her feet and dusting the sand off her butt—but not before he'd seen a glimmer of a grin.

'Nothing's impossible,' he murmured to her retreating back as she marched off in a semi-huff.

He'd got her to agree to manage the biggest campaign of his career—and the one that meant the most. He'd also coerced her into staying with him for a week, and to be his date for the wedding.

Considering how he'd ended things between them all those years ago, he hadn't just pulled off the impossible he'd pulled off a miracle.

* * *

Archer didn't want his family getting wind of his house-guest just yet.

The Christmas Eve wedding would be bad enough without the Flett hordes descending on his place to check her out.

He'd twigged pretty fast that despite Callie being a Melbourne girl she was vastly different from his usual choice of date. She didn't need a truckload of make-up before being seen in the morning, she didn't need a hair-straightener or the name of the nearest manicurist, and she didn't wrinkle her nose at walking on the beach in case her pedicure got chipped.

Maybe he'd made a mistake asking her to be his date for the wedding, because from where he was sitting, staring at the distant dot strolling on the beach, her hair streaming in a dark cloud behind her, he wondered if she'd be enough of a safeguard.

Callie was naturally warm and vibrant, not aloof and standoffish, the way he wanted his women to be when he visited home.

He *liked* that his folks disapproved of his dates and kept their distance. That was the whole point. What if they were drawn to Callie like he was and his plan to keep them at arm's length came crashing down?

He had to keep the Fletts away for as long as possible until the wedding, just in case.

He'd managed to fly under the radar so far. Last night had been spent poring over Callie's ideas for the surf school website, thrashing out slogans and content, working late over homemade pizzas and beer.

It scared him, how comfortable it was having her around. He'd never had a woman stay at his place, let alone lived with anyone. It was his sanctuary, away from the surf crowd, the fans, the media.

No one knew he owned this place except his family.

Some of whom were belting down his door at this very minute.

Damn. So much for keeping their distance.

Cursing under his breath, he yanked the door open and glared at Trav and Tom, ignoring the familiar squeeze his heart gave when he glimpsed Izzy, his six-year-old niece, peering up at him from behind her dad's legs.

He hated how out of all the Fletts she was the one guaranteed to make him feel the worst for staying away. The kid was too young to realise what was going on, but she managed to lay a guilt trip on him every visit.

At three, she'd stuck her tongue out at his date every chance she got and bugged him to teach her how to surf. He'd begged off with his usual excuse—only staying for two days, maybe next time.

At four, she'd placed stick insects in his date's handbag and a hermit crab in her designer shoe, while pestering him for the elusive surf lesson.

At five, she'd verbally flayed his date for her 'too yellow' hair and 'too red' lipstick, and had given up asking him to surf.

He should have been glad. Instead it had ripped him in two when he'd said goodbye to her around this time last year.

It wasn't Izzy's fault he had issues with the rest of his family, but he was scared. Getting close to Izzy might let the rest of them in again, which made him angsty. What if he let them into his heart again only to have it handed back to him like eight years ago?

Every trip home it was the same. Initial tension between him and his brothers soon easing into general ribbing and guy-chat, his mum fussing around him, and prolonged stilted awkwardness with his dad. He still wanted the security of Callie as his buffer zone, but maybe this time he'd swallow his pride and make the first move.

He'd wanted to in the past, but every time he made the decision to broach the gap he'd realise two days weren't long enough to make up for the years apart.

This year he was staying for a week. No excuse.

He squatted down to her level. 'Hey, Iz, long time no see.'

She frowned, but it didn't detract from the curious sparkle in her big blue eyes.

The expression in those eyes—guileless, genuine, trusting—slugged him anew. A guy couldn't hide for long from those eyes. They saw too much, knew too much—including the fact he was acting like a recalcitrant jerk in not welcoming his brothers into his home.

He opened his arms, saw the indecision on her face before she slowly stepped out from behind Tom's legs. She hesitated and his gut squelched with sadness.

It shouldn't be like this—his own niece treating him like a stranger. *He'd* done this, with his stubborn pride. He needed to get over the past. For the longer it took the harder it became to pretend nothing had happened and go back to the way it had been before: a close-knit family who supported each other through everything.

Archer waited, eyeballing Izzy, hoping she could see how much he wanted to squeeze her tight.

After another interminable second that felt like sixty, she flung herself into his arms. He exhaled in relief as he hugged her hard, ignoring the flutter in his chest he got every time this kid wrapped her arms around his neck and hung on as if she'd never let go.

'Where've you been?' She released him, stepped back and crossed her arms as he stood. 'You never come see me any more.'

Practically squirming under the interrogation, Archer floundered for words that wouldn't sound like a trite excuse.

Tom placed a hand on his daughter's shoulder. 'You know your uncle travels a lot, honey. We're lucky to see him when he has time.'

Ouch. Tom's barb slugged him like the punches they'd traded as kids, wrestling at the water's edge to see who'd get the long board for the day.

'At least he always brings me a gift,' Izzy said, pushing her way past him and bounding to the chessboard set up in a far corner, her natural exuberance replacing the reticence that sliced him up inside.

'Manners, Iz,' Tom said, following his daughter into the room and looking around in a not too subtle attempt at sussing out Callie's whereabouts.

'Couldn't keep your big mouth shut, huh?' Archer elbowed Trav as he brought up the rear. 'When we surfed the other day you said you'd keep your lips zipped about me being back early.'

His youngest brother grinned. 'Tom threatened me with bodily harm, and considering he's around a lot more than you, I caved.'

Great—another dig at his absenteeism. Closely following Izzy's reluctant treatment, it made him feel like a heel.

'So where is she?' Tom stuck his hands in his pockets and looked around.

'Who?'

'This mystery woman, of course.' Tom eyeballed him. 'When you make it home for your obligatory Christmas visit your date stays in town. So the fact she's staying here speaks volumes.'

Tom jerked a thumb in Trav's direction. 'We want to check her out, make sure she hasn't got two heads, 'cos that's the only kind of woman who'd be crazy enough to stay here with you.'

Despite another dig from Tom about his obligatory visits, Archer felt his tension fade at his brother's jocularity. 'Wanna beer?'

'Sure.'

Ideally Archer didn't want them hanging around long enough to meet Callie, who'd gone for a walk on the beach to clear her head after a marathon morning brainstorming. But Tom was right; he barely saw his brothers any more and, even though they'd been complicit in his dad's decision to keep the truth secret, he missed the camaraderie they'd once shared.

'I bring a date home every year. This one's no different.' Archer's heart gave a betraying buck at the lie.

'So you're letting some plastic, fake, stick-thin bimbo share your secret hideaway?' Tom snorted. 'Not bloody likely.'

Archer wanted to defend those poor women his brother had just disparaged, but sadly he happened to agree. The women he'd brought home in the past had been exactly as Tom described and not a patch on Callie.

'She's not real, is she? You've made her up so Mum won't go into her speed-dating frenzy in an effort to have you settle for a local girl rather than *those city girls*.'

Archer chuckled at Tom's imitation of their mum, who made *those city girls* sound as if he was dating a brothel's inhabitants.

Tom had followed him into the kitchen, and Archer handed him a beer while uncapping another for Trav and popping an orange soda tab for Izzy.

'She's real. And you'll get to meet her at the wedding like everyone else.'

He held up his beer bottle and Tom clinked it. 'Sure she hasn't got two heads?'

Archer smirked. 'Trust me, Callie's pretty great—'

'Callie? *The* Callie?'

Tom lowered his beer and stared at him with blatant curiosity as Archer silently cursed his slip of the tongue.

He'd had no intention of telling anyone her name until the wedding—let alone Tom, the only Flett who knew how close he'd come to giving up his dream for her.

He'd blurted it out after Tom's divorce had been finalised, sitting on his deck four years ago. That had been one hell of a night. Tom had been miserable, Trav had been blind drunk and clueless how to handle the situation, and Archer had felt like an outcast. The three of them had been in a foul mood and it had almost come to blows. Archer had tussled with Tom and that release of steam and testosterone had opened up a narrow pathway to the truth.

Tom and Trav had told him about dad then—how he'd sworn them to secrecy, how they'd hated keeping it from him but hadn't wanted to stress the seriously ill Frank.

He guessed he understood their logic—who knew? He might have done the same—but it didn't make it any easier to handle when he still didn't know why he'd been the odd man out.

With the air somewhat cleared between them, talk had moved on to Tom's divorce, and Archer had sunk beers in commiseration, alternating between being outraged and bitter on behalf of his brother, who'd done the right thing by marrying the girl he'd got pregnant and yet got screwed over anyway, and determination never to end up like him.

Tom had been morose, berating himself for losing his head over a woman, and Archer had made the mistake of opening up about Callie to make him feel better.

'You're not the only one. We all get sucked in by a memorable female now and then.'

That confession under the onslaught of too many lagers had now come back to bite him on the butt.

He forced a laugh, aiming for casual. 'Turns out my online marketing manager is Callie. Had no idea 'til we met in Melbourne to tee up the surf school campaign. She's here to work for the week—made sense she came to the wedding as my date. Nothing more to it.'

Archer took a slug of beer after his spiel, wondering who he was trying to convince—himself or Tom.

Yesterday had been tough. Hell, it had been sheer torture, watching Callie come alive as she sketched out ideas, seeing her glow as he approved an early pro forma, seeing glimpses of the vibrant woman he'd once lost his head over many years ago.

Sadly she reserved her enthusiasm for work only. Following that impulsive kiss on the beach she'd reverted to coolly polite and casually friendly.

She might have ditched her initial antagonism, but an invisible barrier between them was still there—one he had no hope of breaching considering how things had ended between them.

Correction: how *he'd* ended things between them.

He didn't blame her for being wary. But late last night, with the woman he'd once been crazy for sleeping in the room next door and insomnia plaguing him, he'd wished they could recapture half the easy-going camaraderie they'd once shared.

He only had a week to get this surf school campaign up and running before he flew out to Hawaii for Christmas Day, so realistically he couldn't afford to stuff around.

He knew what he was doing. Flirting with her as a deliberate tactic to distract himself from the stress of being home and having to deal with his family. It was a distancing technique he'd honed with other dates before her. But none had affected him as much as Callie.

He'd deliberately kept things between them light-hearted and work-focussed, but what would happen if he ratcheted up the heat? Would she release some of that new reserve she carried around like an invisible cloak and resurrect the passion they'd once shared?

Tom pointed his beer in Archer's direction. 'The fact she's the first woman you've ever brought here speaks volumes.'

'It was convenient for work, that's all.'

'Yeah, keep telling yourself that.'

Or course Callie chose that moment to hustle through the back door, wind-tousled and pink-cheeked and utterly delectable.

'Hey, Arch, there's a car out front—' She caught sight of Tom and stopped, her eyes widening, before she crossed the kitchen and held out her hand. 'You're a much better-looking version of Archer, so you must be a Flett too.'

Tom laughed as he shook her hand. 'I like her already,' he said, while Archer shot him a filthy look.

'Callie, meet my older brother, Tom.'

A playful smile teased the corners of her mouth as she glanced up at Tom—a smile she hadn't shot *him* once since they'd arrived.

'Pleased to meet you.'

Something painful twisted in his chest at the way she lit up in the way she'd once used to light up around him.

'Come meet his daughter—and Trav, the groom.'

Tom's goofy grin proved what he already knew: he sounded like an uptight ass.

'You have a little girl? That's great,' Callie said, falling into step beside Tom while Archer brought up the rear, hating himself for feeling petty and out of sorts that Callie had lightened up for the first time since yesterday because of his brother.

'Hey, another girl. Awesome.'

Izzy flew at Callie and a strange, unidentifiable feeling swamped him as he watched his niece hug her, spontaneously and without reserve, the way he'd wished Iz had hugged *him* when he'd first opened the door.

Unfazed, Callie led Izzy back to the chessboard, where she shook hands with Trav, whose goofy grin matched Tom's.

Great—two Flett males she'd slayed. He couldn't wait until she met his dad.

Three.

The number popped into his head.

Three Flett males she'd slayed, including him. No matter how many times he denied it, the fact remained: Callie was the kind of woman who could have an impact on a guy.

An unforgettable impact, considering the schmuck he turned into around her.

When he finally tore his gaze away from the captivating sight of Callie giggling alongside Izzy, Tom's smug smirk greeted him.

'So tell me. What did an amazing woman like that see in a putz like you? And why the hell did you let her go?'

Did.

Past tense.

Having his brother verbalise what he'd been wondering himself since reconnecting with her ticked him off more than the uncertainty plaguing him.

This week was about work and familial obligation, before he fled back to the life he liked. If a little light-hearted flirtation with Callie made it more bearable, so be it.

He hadn't banked on this restlessness, this annoying

feeling that he was missing out on something by making the lifestyle choices he had. Worse, having his brother articulate it.

'Leave it alone,' he muttered under his breath, garnering a broader grin from Tom.

'You know I'm the last person to believe in all that romance crap, considering the number Tracy did on me, but have you ever considered this coincidence of her coming back into your life might mean something?'

Archer stared at his brother in amazement. Tom had given up his dreams to turn pro for Tracy, a local surf groupie who'd deliberately got pregnant to snare her man. Tom had foregone his dream to marry Tracy, stay in Torquay and raise Izzy.

Ironically, Tracy had been the one to take off a year into the marriage, leaving Tom with a toddler and a nagging bitterness.

Tom didn't believe in happily-ever-afters, so the fact he'd mentioned the word *romance* and alluded to fate alerted Archer to how badly he must be making a fool of himself.

'You've been spending too much time reading Izzy's fairytales, mate.' His gruff response came out as a snarl, and he immediately realised his reaction had increased rather than eased Tom's suspicions.

Tom held up his hands. 'Just voicing an impartial opinion. No need to get your tether rope in a knot.'

Callie pumped her fists in the air and shimmied her shoulders as Trav made a disastrous move with his queen. Izzy cheered and Callie joined in, her vivacity flooring him in a way he'd never expected.

She'd been so focussed yesterday, concentrating on business and little else. He'd forgotten she could be like this: funny and vibrant and cute.

Well, not forgotten exactly; the memories had been deliberately shoved to a far recess of his mind and ignored. It wouldn't be good for him to recall how good they'd been together for that brief time in Capri. It would only end in tears.

Archer glared at Tom. 'You breathe one word of her staying here to the folks and you're dead.'

A cunning glint lit Tom's eyes. 'Tell you what. I'll keep my mouth shut if you admit you still want her.'

In response, Archer got him in a headlock. He could never stay detached with Trav or Tom for long. Each year when he returned his initial aloofness disappeared a little quicker.

Besides, he didn't really blame them for withholding stuff he should have been privy to. That had been his dad's doing and, while he loved the stubborn old coot, he couldn't forget. Forgive? Yeah, he'd done that a few years back. Now he just had to pluck up the courage to let Frank know, rather than punishing him because he couldn't get the words out to make it all better.

As he tussled with Tom, Izzy joined in the fun by leaping on her dad's back. Her squeals of laughter didn't distract him from the truth.

Denying any semblance of feeling for Callie was useless.

She'd wheedled her way under his skin.

Again.

And there wasn't one damn thing he could do about it.

CHAPTER FIVE

'PEACE at last.' Archer slid Callie a coffee as she lounged on the balcony.

'Your brothers are cool and Izzy's adorable,' Callie said, adding an extra spoon of sugar to her espresso.

She needed the hit, still reeling from seeing Archer in a family environment. The guy she'd known had never talked about family. He had been the quintessential loner who breezed through life without a care in the world. The guy who didn't commit to anything or anyone beyond his beloved surfing.

So to see him interacting with his brothers had thrown her. He'd been reserved at first, as if he didn't want them in his home—which made no sense after the rough-housing she'd seen once he'd lightened up.

When she'd strolled into the kitchen after her walk it had been like walking smack-bang into an invisible glass wall. The tension had been that thick. She'd glimpsed the circumspection in his eyes and the fact she'd recognised it, could get a read on his feelings after all this time, had irked.

She'd masked her discomfort by being bright and bubbly and a little gushing with his brothers and niece. Which had seemed to annoy Archer further.

What was wrong with the guy? As his date for the wedding, didn't he want her to act naturally around his family? *Sheesh.*

And that was another thing that had thrown her: his obvious attachment to his niece. He'd never struck her as the type to like kids. Not with his lifestyle. But he'd been smitten with Izzy, and seeing the two of them together, their heads bent close as they mulled over a jigsaw puzzle, had unlocked a host of feelings she'd rather not deal with.

She didn't want to remember how attentive and caring he'd been in Capri. And she sure as hell didn't want to acknowledge his consistent flirting, slowly chipping away at her necessary resistance.

She wouldn't give in—not when she knew his overt displays of charm came as naturally to him as catching a wave. She'd been sucked in by it once, and had been let down beyond belief.

She knew that feeling well. Bruno Umberto had made an art form of building up hopes only to let down his daughter.

As for the rare glimpses of unguarded admiration—first when she'd been playing chess with Trav, then when she'd made lemonade for Izzy—she didn't like that at all.

He'd used to look at her like that in Capri, as if she were the only woman in the world, and to see the same look seriously perturbed her. She couldn't afford to get involved with Archer again—not when her emotions were already bruised and fragile from the rollercoaster ride with her mum.

Living life in the moment was one thing. Setting herself up for another dose of heartbreak was another.

She'd given in to his request to be his wedding date for one reason only: to keep the peace between them so they could get the surf school business done and dusted this week.

That kiss on the beach had been just like the one in the car on the way down here yesterday morning. Archer being Archer. Impulsive. Rash. Selfish. Doing what he wanted regardless of the consequences.

Harsh? Maybe, but all the kisses in the world couldn't turn back time and erase the way he'd ended things between them, and that was what she had to focus on if she were to keep any residual feelings at bay.

And doing that was imperative. She couldn't afford to acknowledge how incredible his kisses were, how alive they made her feel.

Uh-uh. She needed to focus on the one reason she was here: business.

'Yeah, Izzy's the best.' Archer held up a hand, wavered it. 'Tom and Trav? Not so much.'

'Your mum must've had a handful with three boys.'

He stiffened, as if she'd asked an intensely personal question rather than making conversation. 'Yeah, we kept her on her toes.'

She wanted to ask about his parents, about his childhood, but she couldn't get a read on his mood.

They were sprawled on comfy cushioned sofas—she'd studiously avoided the love-seat—on the glass-enclosed balcony, overlooking an amazing ocean tinged with sunset. It reeked of intimacy, yet Archer's perfunctory answers and shuttered expression weren't encouraging.

'Do you want kids?'

And then he went and floored her with a question like that. A question far surpassing intimacy and heading straight for uncomfortable.

'Not sure.'

She cradled her coffee cup, hoping some if its warmth would melt the icy tentacles of unease squeezing her heart.

After the genetic testing, when it had been proved she

didn't have the mutated gene that sounded a death knell for her mum, she'd undergone counselling to get a grip on her rioting emotions: relief, guilt, happiness, fear. Yet for all these years, deep down where she hid her innermost fears, she hadn't been able to shake the irrational dread that somehow those doctors had made a mistake and she'd contract the disease after all.

Crazy and illogical. The odds were in her favour to have perfectly healthy kids. But why tempt fate when it had dealt her such a rough hand so far?

'The opportunity hasn't come up?'

Surprised by his line of questioning, she eyeballed him. 'If you're asking if I've been in a serious relationship since Capri, no. I've dated. That's about it.'

She half expected him to flinch at her bluntness in bringing up the past, but to his credit he didn't look away.

'Why?'

'What is this? Pry into Callie's soul day?'

She placed her coffee on the nearest table and her hands unexpectedly shook.

'Callie, I—'

'Sorry for snapping your head off, but if you're hoping to hear I've been pining for you all these years, and that's why I'm not involved in a serious relationship, you're delusional.'

His eyes widened in horror. 'Hell, that's not what I want.' He rubbed the back of his neck in a familiar gesture that added to the poignancy of the moment. 'I just feel like we've been doing this avoidance dance, concentrating on work, making polite small talk, retreating to our rooms. Then I saw how you were with Izzy and it got me thinking...'

She shouldn't ask. She really shouldn't. 'About?'

Yep, she was asking for it.

'About why the beautiful, vibrant woman I met in Capri hasn't been snapped up by some smart guy?'

A guy smarter than you? she wanted to say, but silently counted to five before she blurted it out.

'Maybe I don't want to be snapped up? Maybe I'm happy with my life the way it is?'

'Are you?'

She stiffened as he reached out and traced a fingertip between her brows, eliciting a shiver.

'Because you've got this little dent here that tells me otherwise.'

Touched he'd noticed, annoyed at his intuitiveness, she swatted his hand away. 'How did you get so perceptive?'

'Honestly?'

She picked up her coffee cup, cradled it, hiding behind it as she took a deep sip and nodded.

'The way you lit up around Izzy was the same way you used to be in Capri. Carefree. Quick to laugh. Like nothing fazed you.' He paused, as if searching her face for approval to continue. 'At first I thought it was me and the way I treated you in the past that was bugging you. But it's something else—something that runs deeper.'

He snaffled her hand and squeezed it before she could protest.

'You know you can tell me, right?'

Uh-oh. Callie could handle teasing, charming Archer. She couldn't handle this newer, sensitive version, who'd honed in on the emotional load she carried daily like an invisible yoke.

'We should finish off the home page of the website—'

He gripped her hand tighter. 'Tell me.'

'Wow, you're bossy.' She blew out a long, slow breath, not wanting to do this but knowing he'd keep badgering until she did.

He'd been like that in Capri: badgering her to have dinner with him that first night; badgering her to stroll along the moonlit beach afterwards; badgering her with his loaded stares and sexy smiles and wicked ways.

Now, like then, she was powerless to resist.

'It's my mum. She has motor neurone disease.'

Shock widened his eyes and sadness twisted his mouth. 'Aw, honey, I'm sorry.'

'Me too,' she said, gnawing on her bottom lip and willing the sudden sting of tears away.

She'd cried enough to fill the Tasman Sea but it didn't change the facts. The horrid disease was eating away at her mum's nervous system one neurone at a time.

'There's nothing they can do?'

She shook her head, grateful for the strong hold he had on her hand. She would have bolted for the sanctity of her room otherwise and not come out for the next few days.

'They initially gave her three years. She's lasted seven.'

Quick as ever he did the math, and understanding flickered in those aquamarine depths. 'Did you find out soon after you got home from Europe?'

She nodded, remembering the far-reaching consequences of that diagnosis.

Despite the way they'd ended, would she have booked a flight to join Archer if her mum hadn't fallen ill? Would her life have been filled with sunshine and sand and surf rather than a rented box-like office space? Would she have been blissfully unaware of the potential gene landmine pumping through her veins and had Archer's kids?

Stupid thinking, considering Archer hadn't wanted her back then, let alone a commitment that could lead to kids.

'So she's undergoing the usual rounds of physiotherapy and occupational therapy to keep her as mobile as possible?'

'Yeah, though her muscle wastage is advancing pretty rapidly.'

How many times had she gently massaged those muscles in the hope they'd somehow miraculously regenerate? Too many. The sight of Nora wasting away before her eyes broke her heart.

'She's confined to a wheelchair, though the special home where she lives is fabulous in taking care of her.'

'The staff in those facilities deserve a medal, considering the range of healthcare they provide.'

'How come you know so much about it?'

'I sponsored a charity benefit for Lou Gehrig's disease in LA. Thought I'd better know something about it before rocking up to the shindig.'

Callie eyed him speculatively. Sportsmen around the world attended charity benefits, but she doubted many of them cared enough to delve into the details of the fundraiser's disease.

'Is there anything I can do?'

Touched he'd offered, she shook her head. 'Thanks, but I've got it covered.'

At least she would have once she got paid for this surf school campaign. Which meant getting back to work, despite the urge to linger in this intimate cocoon where the guy she'd once loved seriously cared.

'We should get back to work—'

'Tomorrow,' he said, scooting alongside her and draping an arm across her shoulders before she had a chance to move. 'We've been pushing it pretty hard since we arrived yesterday. Let's just chill tonight.'

Chilling sounded good, but sadly there was nothing cool about being snuggled in the crook of Archer's shoulder. The opposite, with her body warming from the inside out until it felt as if her skin blistered.

She should move, should head inside and collate a few more ideas for the website's link page. Instead she found herself slowly relaxing into him, wanting to savour this moment.

The irony of being cradled in Archer's arms after she'd rammed home the fact that this week was just about business wasn't lost on her. It felt good. Great, in fact. But temporary—a comforting hug from an ex. An ex who'd ended their all-too-brief relationship in no uncertain terms.

She wouldn't get used to it, but for now, with his solid warmth seeping through her, she couldn't help but wonder what it would be like if she made the most of their remaining time together.

Was she a glutton for punishment to contemplate another short-term fling? Heck, yeah. But considering the road ahead—the uncertainty of her mum's illness, her lifespan, and the ensuing pain when the inevitable happened—would it be so bad to take a little bit of happiness while she could?

Logically, she'd be an idiot to contemplate it.

Emotionally, her heart strained towards him, eager for affection, knowing how sensational they could be together even for a scant week.

He kissed the top of her head and she sighed, appreciating his sensitivity in not pushing her to talk any more.

Besides, she'd said enough. She hadn't told any of her past dates about her mum—hadn't let them get close enough. Yet in two days she'd let Archer march back into her life—and a little corner of her heart if she were completely honest—and trusted him enough to divulge the truth about her mum.

At least she hadn't told him all of it. Some things were best left unsaid.

The memory of her genetic testing sent a shiver through

her and he tightened his hold, conveying strength in silence.

Yeah, she could do worse than have some fun for a change over the next week.

In the lead-up to Christmas surely she'd been a good girl all year and Santa owed her big-time?

The next morning Callie had to admit spending the week in Torquay had been a stroke of genius on Archer's part.

She'd worked uninterrupted for the last three hours, perched on his balcony, enjoying the sea air and the view, inspired in a way she hadn't been for a long time.

She didn't know if it was being away from the office for the first time in years that had sparked her creativity, but she'd added some amazing touches to the surf school website today. Ideas to build on when he gave her the grand tour this afternoon.

It helped that he'd made himself scarce since dawn this morning. She hadn't been looking forward to having him hover over her workspace after her confession last night.

Sure, it had seemed as if telling him about her mum had been the right thing to do at the time, while they were relaxed and cosy at dusk, but in the harsh light of day, after a sleepless night spent second-guessing herself, she hadn't wanted to face him.

Shared confidences bred intimacy, and that was one thing she couldn't afford with Archer. She'd been foolish enough in testing herself by being here this week. For while he'd demanded she come to Torquay to secure the campaign she probably could have weaselled her way out of it if she'd tried.

But the moment he'd strutted into her office, spouting his terms, she'd wanted to prove to herself once and for all that she was over him, that he had no hold over her despite spending seven days in her company.

She'd been doing a good job of it too—those kisses he'd sprung on her notwithstanding—until last night.

Following their break-up, she'd tarred Archer with the same brush as her dad: selfish, self-absorbed, a man who followed his whims without regard to anyone else. It had been a coping mechanism, labelling him so harshly.

Yet last night—the way he'd comforted her, the way he'd been attuned to her mood and content to sit in silence—had seriously undermined her lowly opinion of him and made her seem childish in lashing out in the past because she'd been foolish enough to feel more than he had.

Laughter drifted up from the beach and she sheltered her eyes with her hand to focus on the group by the water's edge.

A bunch of teenagers surrounded Archer, their boards stuck vertically in the sand like sentinels. He stood in the centre, gesturing towards the ocean, demonstrating a few moves, while the teens jostled and elbowed for prime position in front of their idol.

Embarrassment twanged her heart. A selfish guy wouldn't give up his precious school-set-up time to hang with a bunch of kids. Just as a selfish guy wouldn't have taken the time to comfort her last night.

Feeling increasingly guilty, she shut down the webpage program she'd been tweaking, scooped up her paperwork and dumped the lot inside.

Another bonus of working here. She could take a head-clearing walk along the beach any time. And right now, remorseful, she wanted to let Archer know he wasn't so bad after all.

Not that she had any intention of confessing such a thing to him, but she'd been pretty remote, deliberately maintaining an invisible distance between them. Considering how great he'd been with her last night, it wouldn't hurt for her to lighten up a tad.

She slipped off her sandals at the bottom of the steps, loving the gritty sand squelching between her toes as she strolled towards him.

The closer she got, the more she could see the rapt expressions on the teens' faces, and hear Archer giving a pep talk. The guy was usually a livewire, but she'd never seen him so animated. Which made her wonder why he'd been so reticent with his brothers when he was obviously a people person.

The pep talk must have worked because the teens let out a rousing cheer before grabbing their boards and heading for the surf.

Archer's eyes glowed with pride and satisfaction as he waved her over.

'Did you see that?'

She smiled and nodded. 'Those kids think you're a surf god.'

'I just gave them a few pointers. But the way they responded…' He shook his head, staring at the wetsuited blobs bobbing in the ocean. 'They were blown away to hear about the surf school and asked a million questions. They're going to tell their mates.'

He pumped his fist. 'I'm stoked.'

'You did good.' She touched his arm, an impulsive gesture to convey her approval, but one she regretted when he snagged her hand and tugged her close.

'Your approval means a lot.'

'Why?' She eased away, needing to put a little distance between them, overwhelmed by his closeness.

'Because I hate to have you think badly of me.'

Still wrestling with her recent revelation as to his true

character, she aimed for levity. 'Come this time next week it won't matter what I think. You'll be hanging loose in Hawaii or Bali, and I'll be doing an amazing job maintaining your surf school website.'

'You're wrong.'

She pretended to misunderstand. 'No, really, I'll be working like a maniac on your website—'

'Your opinion matters.'

She glanced away, unable to fathom his steady stare, almost daring her to—what? Argue? Agree? Analyse?

'Aren't you going to ask me why?'

She bit down on her bottom lip. No, she didn't want to hear any of the deep and meaningful reasons he'd concocted. However much she regretted misjudging him all these years, she didn't want anything from this week beyond a successful campaign.

'Fine. I'll tell you anyway.' He released her arm, only to capture her chin, leaving her no option but to look at him. 'You're the only woman I've ever known who gets me. And, while it scares the hell out of me, I kinda think it's cool.'

Oh, heck. Trapped beneath the intensity of his stare, with his praise like a soft caress, she felt the inevitable pull between them flare to life.

She couldn't look away, couldn't resist as their lips inched towards each other, couldn't think of a rational reason why she shouldn't kiss an old flame on a pristine beach.

Old flame… Those two words penetrated her dazed fog.

What the heck was she doing? She could blame his first two kisses on impulse, but this? This was something else entirely.

If her opinion mattered to him, his praise mattered to

her. She basked under his admiration, but letting it go to her head would be beyond foolhardy.

She couldn't do this. Fall under his spell. *Again.*

She wasn't the same naïve girl any more. This time she had no doubt if they had another fling it would end the same way.

All the whispered words in the world wouldn't change the facts: Archer lived for his freedom; she lived for making Nora's lifespan—what was left of it—as comfortable as possible.

Their goals were worlds apart.

With their lips almost touching, she wrenched out of his grasp and took a few backward steps.

'Callie—'

She couldn't bear the confusion warring with something deeper in his eyes, so she did the only thing possible.

She turned and ran.

CHAPTER SIX

'WHAT do you think?'

Callie stared at Archer's 'little' surf school, not quite comprehending how the plans and architectural impressionist photos she'd used for the pre-website had morphed into this sprawling complex perched on a sheltered bluff metres from the ocean.

'It's absolutely breathtaking,' she said, doing a three-sixty, taking in the whitewashed main building, the dorms with bright blue doors, the storeroom large enough to house her apartment three times over, and the supplies shop tucked to the left of the entrance.

'You designed all this?'

His mouth quirked. 'Don't sound so incredulous. I'm not just a pretty face.'

She grimaced at his lame line. He laughed. 'Come on, I'll give you the grand tour.'

He snagged her hand as if it was the most natural thing in the world, and she clamped down on her first urge to ease it away.

She'd done some hard thinking after she'd bolted from the beach earlier. Confiding in Archer about her mum's illness last night, allowing him to hold her, welcoming his comfort, followed by their closeness on the beach that morning, had solidified what she'd already known deep down.

That spending time with him, albeit for work, had the potential to crack open the protective wall she'd erected around her heart.

The fissures had appeared with his kisses, and they'd well and truly fractured last night, when they'd sat on that damned deck until the sun set. Throw in that *moment* on the beach today and…trouble.

That was another thing. He'd been quiet last night, attuned to her need for silence while still holding her. He hadn't prattled on with small talk designed to distract. He'd just held her, his arm wrapped solidly around her waist, his cheek resting lightly on the top of her head.

He thought she *got* him? The feeling was entirely mutual and that was scarier than any reawakening feelings she might be experiencing.

He'd been like that in Capri—attuned to her moods and desires after only just meeting. It was as if they'd fitted. She didn't believe in love at first sight, or great loves, or romantic kismet—her pragmatic mum and selfish dad had ensured that—but her connection with Archer eight years earlier had defied logic.

He'd anticipated what she'd wanted back then—more Chianti, a cotton shawl for their evening walk, another swim—but his intuition beyond the physical had impressed her the most.

He'd tuned in to her emotionally, on some deeper level that had made her truly comfortable with him in a way she'd never been with another guy. They'd talked for hours. Usually about inconsequential stuff, childhood anecdotes, secret dreams, and she'd never recaptured that magic with any date.

It had made their break up all the harder.

They'd both had open-ended travel tickets and hadn't discussed moving on. While the end of their holiday idyll had been inevitable, she'd expected to stay in contact. And a small part of her had hoped they'd reconnect in Melbourne one day.

But all that had ended when he'd told her the blunt truth: she'd read too much into a holiday fling. What they'd shared was nothing more than a bit of fun and she needed to lighten up before she scared off more guys.

His harsh words had hurt. Devastated her, in fact, and she'd never understood how the guy she'd grown so close to in such a short space of time could shut down emotionally and walk away without looking back.

She'd do well to remember the past before those cracks and fissures around her heart disintegrated completely.

Thankfully he hadn't mentioned her bolt up the beach after their almost-kiss, and she'd been working double time to pretend everything was fine.

She'd finish out this week without him knowing how he still affected her if it killed her.

She pointed at a sign with her free hand. 'I still can't believe you called it Winki Pop Surf School. Sounds like something out of a kid's fairytale.'

He feigned indignation. 'I'll have you know Winki Pop is one of the best surf breaks around here.' He chuckled. 'Besides, it has a better ring to it than some of the other breaks around here.'

'Like?'

'Southside. Centreside. Rincon.'

'I see your point. It does have a certain charm.'

''Course it would, with me as the owner.' He winked. 'Mr Winki, that's me.'

She groaned at his terrible joke, his carefree laughter

reminding her of another time they'd swapped banter like this, a time she'd treasured before reality set in.

She listened closely as they toured the school, taking mental notes. The smart thing to do would be take out her iPhone and dictate ideas, or pull out the trusty notepad she kept in her bag.

But both activities would involve releasing Archer's hand, and for now her blasé act depended on it. Easing her hand out of his would probably have him asking what was wrong, and if it was connected to earlier on the beach, and yada, yada, yada. She just didn't want to go there.

When they reached the store shed he unlocked the door and flung it open. 'Ready to put the master touch on the online forums you suggested?'

Confused, she glanced inside the shed lined with surfboards and wetsuits of all shapes and sizes. 'Not sure what you mean.'

His wicked grin alerted her to an incoming suggestion she wouldn't like.

'If you're going to be the moderator of the school's online forums, you need to know what it feels like to surf.'

The incoming missile detonated and left her reeling. 'Me? On a surfboard? Out *there*?' Her voice ended on a squeak as she pointed to the expanse of ocean a short stroll away.

'Yeah. And no better time to start than now.'

Like hell. She loved swimming, loved the ocean, but no way would she klutz around like a floundering whale in front of him. Learning to surf had always been on her life's 'to do' list, but here, now, with *him*?

No flipping way.

She snapped her fingers. 'Sorry, no bathers. Maybe next time—'

'I'm sure we stock your size.'

His gaze roved her body, assessing, warming, zinging every nerve-ending along the way.

Before she could protest further he placed a hand in the small of her back and propelled her forward.

'Come on. You said surfing was on your bucket list. No time like the present to tick it off while getting first-hand experience for work.'

Stunned he'd remembered her bucket list, she allowed him to lead her into the dim interior.

A pungent blend of new fibreglass, rubber and coconut-scented wax tickled her nose, but through all that she could smell the potent male beside her: sunshine and sea air and pure Archer.

He was right, of course. Knowing what learning to surf entailed would give her more credibility when she manned the surf school online forums, so technically this classi-fied as work.

But the part where he sized up her body, his glance as intimate as a lover's caress, went beyond work. Way beyond.

Her skin grew clammy as he flicked through the suits on a rack before unhooking a black wetsuit with a fuchsia zig-zag and handing it to her.

'Here—this should fit.'

A little tremor of excitement shot through her as her fingertips brushed the rubber. How long since she'd done something spontaneous and fun and just for her? Too long. And as he handed her a practical navy one-piece, she sud-denly couldn't wait to get out there.

He jerked a thumb over his shoulder. 'Changing rooms back there. But first let's get you set up with a board.'

'Whatever you choose will be fine.'

He folded his arms, making his biceps bulge beneath the

trendily frayed ends of his designer teal T-shirt. 'Don't you want to get a feel for the board in here before we head out?'

Feeling one hundred percent novice, she wrinkled her nose. 'Um, I'm guessing I'm supposed to say yes?'

'Yeah. You need to connect with your board.'

'Oh, brother,' she muttered, rolling her eyes as they moved across to the other side of the shed, where boards stood vertically in racks. 'Next you'll be making that hand sign and telling me to hang loose.'

He smirked. 'The *shaka* sign is part of surf culture.'

She extended her thumb and little finger while keeping the middle fingers curled. 'So does this make me cool?'

'Nah. You have to stay on a board longer than thirty seconds for that.'

She laughed, watching him run his hands over the boards, sliding down the smooth surfaces, his rapt expression almost making her jealous.

He'd once looked at her like that.

Before he bolted without a backward glance.

She'd do well to remember that rather than wishing she were a surfboard right about now.

'This one.' He slid a monstrous cream board etched in ochre swirls from the rack. 'This is your board.'

'Did the fibreglass speak to you?'

His eyes narrowed in indignation. 'Are you mocking me?'

'A little.'

'Let's see who mocks who when you're face-planting the waves,' he said, beckoning her closer. 'Here, you hold it.'

The thing weighed a tonne, but she managed to hold it upright—just. 'Feels like this thing's made of stone.'

'The best epoxy resin, actually, which makes it stronger

and lighter than traditional boards.' He took hold of her hand and ran it down the board. 'This is called the deck.'

He edged her hand towards the side of the board in a long, slow sweep that made her bite her lip to stop groaning out loud.

There was something so sensual about having him stand close, his body radiating heat, warming her back, his arms outstretched and inadvertently wrapping around her, his large fingers splayed across hers as they'd once splayed across her belly.

She swallowed and prayed he didn't expect an answer, for there wasn't a hope she could speak with her throat constricted.

Her heart pounded like a jackhammer, the blood coursed through her body like liquid wildfire.

The heat suffocated her, making breathing difficult, making thinking impossible, making her crave the insane…him shoving the board aside, ripping off her clothes, and taking her right here, right now, on the sandy floor.

'The back is the tail, the forward tip is the nose, and the side edges are the rails.' He guided her hand back to the middle and she swayed a little. 'The concave surface from nose to tail is the rocker.'

He moved the board side to side and she almost whimpered.

She must have made some giveaway sound, because he wrapped his arms around her from behind, making holding the board steady impossible.

She could feel his heat, feel how much he wanted her pressed up against her, and she'd never felt the urge to forget sanity as much as she did at that moment.

Correction. She'd experienced the same insanity the first night they'd met—the night he'd romanced her and charmed her and convinced her that tumbling into bed in the early hours of the morning, with the Capri moonlight spilling over them and accentuating the beautiful craziness of the night, was the only possible thing she wanted.

Which begged the question…what did she want now?

While her mind tussled with the dilemma, her body gave a resounding response by leaning back into him.

She heard his sharp intake of breath, felt his arms stiffen.

She had no idea how long they stayed like that, suspended for an incredibly tension-fraught moment in time, and if it hadn't for the beep of her darn phone indicating she had a message she had a fair idea of what might have happened.

'Better get that in case it's about Mum,' she said, instantly missing his warmth as he released her and stepped away, managing to hold the board upright and disentangle herself from her simultaneously.

'I'll meet you outside when you're done,' he said, his voice husky and laced with the same passion pumping through her veins as he picked up the boards as if they weighed nothing and marched outside.

With a sigh of regret she shook her head to clear it, fished her phone out of her pocket and checked it. The message from a client could have waited.

This all-consuming yearning, making her want to run after Archer and drag him back to the sanctity of this shed to finish what they'd started, was not so patient.

Torn between wanting to indulge her newly awakened cravings and wanting to slap herself upside the head, she marched over to the change rooms.

The sooner she got back behind the safety of her computer screen and away from sexy surfer, the better.

* * *

Archer jammed the surfboards into the sand and took off for the ocean at a run.

He needed the clarity only the sea could bring. And the chill to ease his inexorable desire.

He'd had a close call back there. So close to giving in to the relentless drive to possess Callie again, to see if the resurfacing memories were half as good as he remembered.

Who was he trying to kid? Those hazy memories were becoming sharper by the day. Even the most trivial things, like watching Callie snag her hair into a ponytail or jot down notes, would resurrect memories of how she'd done the same thing years ago, and he'd be catapulted back to a time when they'd had no responsibilities, no pressures, and were free to indulge their passion.

A time he'd deliberately screwed up to avoid feeling the same way he had when he'd discovered his family had withheld the truth about his dad: as if he wasn't good enough.

He'd trusted his family and they'd let him down, seriously interfering with his ability to trust anyone.

If he couldn't trust them, who could he trust?

Walking away from Callie back then had been inevitable. Early days in a burgeoning career taking him straight to the top. So when she'd got too close, when he'd started to think beyond Capri, when those trust issues had raised their ugly head, it had been easier to sabotage and run without looking back.

That didn't stop him wanting to have that time again.
Now.

The waves broke around his ankles as he sprinted into the sea and dived through the break, the invigorating brace of cold water slicing through his musings but doing little to obliterate his need for her.

He should have known this blasé flirting as a ploy to distract himself from the impending catch-up with his folks would morph into something more.

He had a feeling nothing would dull this ache for Callie. Nothing less than indulging in a mind-blowing physical encounter designed to slake his thirst and get this thing out of his system.

He could have damped down his need, could have kept things friendly and continued on his casual flirting way, if she hadn't blown his mind in the shed.

She wanted this too.

She'd had a choice and she'd made it, leaning back into him, pressing against him, showing him she felt the buzz too.

He'd been stunned, considering the way she'd aborted their kiss a few hours ago. This time, why had *he* bolted?

As he sliced through the water, free-styling as if he had a shark on his tail, he knew.

Last night, when she'd divulged all that heavy stuff about her mum and he'd held her for ages comforting her, he'd started to feel something. He'd felt that sitting on the deck of his home for ages, with a woman he seriously cared about, content to just sit and not talk, was kind of nice.

It was the first time he'd ever been in Torquay and felt like staying. And that terrified him more than any Great White. He wasn't a stayer. Even for a woman with doe eyes and a soft touch.

He rolled onto his back, letting the swell take him. He closed his eyes, savouring the sun warming his body.

This was where he felt at home. In the ocean, with all the time in the world to float, far from people he'd trusted who hadn't returned the favour.

This was where he belonged.

Then why the urgent pull, like a rip dragging him where he didn't want to go, that said belonging to Callie mightn't be so bad after all?

Callie felt like a trussed-up turkey in the wetsuit. She hated the way the rubber stuck to her skin. She hated the way it moulded and delineated every incriminating bump, and she particularly hated how it made her feel.

Like a novice floundering way out of her depth.

She didn't like floundering. She liked staying in control and staying on top and staying in charge.

She'd lost control once before. And the reason was staring at her with blatant appreciation as she trudged towards him.

'By your foul expression, I'm guessing a wisecrack about rubber and being protected isn't in my best interests?'

She glared at him. 'I'm here under sufferance and you damn well know it.'

She could have sworn he muttered, 'You weren't suffering in the shed,' but didn't want to call him on it.

She didn't need a reminder of the heat they'd generated in the shed. Not if she wanted to stay upright on this stupid piece of fibreglass for more than two seconds.

Errant, erotic thoughts of Archer were guaranteed wipe-out material.

She yelped as something brushed her ankle—only to discover Archer grinning up at her.

'How about a crack about keeping a wild woman on a leash?'

She let him fasten the cord attached to the board around her ankle before nudging him away with her foot. 'How about I crack you over the head with one of those boards?'

He laughed, straightened, and unkinked his back.

'Just trying to get you to loosen up.' He added a few side stretches. 'The looser you are, the easier it'll be to get the feel of balancing on the board.'

'I'm loose.'

She took a step and tripped over the leash in the process. His hand shot out to grab her, and even through the rubber his touch sent a lick of heat through her.

'You okay?'

An embarrassed blush flushed her cheeks. 'Let's do this.'

Concern tinged his glance before determination hardened his mouth, and she wondered if this was his game face—the one he used pre-competition. If so, she wasn't surprised he'd won the world championship five times.

He pointed towards the sea. 'We're in luck. Surf's up today and the waves are off the hook.' She raised an eyebrow and he winced. 'Habit. Surf-speak for the waves being a good size and shape.'

'Gnarly dude,' she muttered, earning a rueful grin.

'We'll concentrate on the basics today, and see if we can catch a wave or two.'

Basics sounded good to her. Basics wouldn't involve tubes or rips or drowning, right?

'I'll break it down into steps and you copy, okay?'

She nodded and he dropped down on the board on his front, leaving her with a pretty great view of a rubber-moulded butt.

'You'll need to be in this position to paddle out.'

Got it, she thought. *Paddling...butt...*

'Cal? You planning on joining me down here?'

With an exasperated grunt at her attention span—not entirely her fault, considering the distraction on offer—she lowered herself onto the board and imitated paddling.

'Nice action,' he said, and her head snapped up to check for the slightest hint of condescension.

Instead she caught him staring in the same vicinity she'd been looking at a moment ago, and a thrill of womanly pride shot through her.

'Next is the pop-up.' He demonstrated going from lying on his board to standing, all in one jump. 'And gaining your balance.'

He held his arms out to his sides, looking so perfectly natural on the board it was as if it was an extension of his feet.

'Now you try.'

And try she did. Over and over again. Until her arms, knees and back ached from her lousy pop-ups and her pride absolutely smarted.

Though she had to hand it to him. Archer was a patient teacher. He praised and cajoled and criticised when needed, eventually getting her from the sand into the water. Where the fun really began.

'Don't worry if you get caught inside,' he said, paddling alongside her.

'Huh?' she mouthed, concentrating on keeping her belly on the board so she didn't slip off as the swell buffeted.

'It's when a surfer paddles out and can't get past the breaking surf to the calmer part of the ocean to catch a wave.'

'Right.' She tried a salute and almost fell off the board.

'If you do, you can try to duck-dive by pushing the nose of the board under the oncoming wave, but it's probably easier just to coast back into shore and we'll try again later.'

She nodded, knowing there wouldn't be a 'later'. She reckoned she had enough first-hand experience now to facilitate the online forums. Perching on top of a wave wouldn't give her much more beyond a momentary rush of adrenalin.

'Follow me.'

And she did. Until she got caught inside, just as he'd predicted, and ended up paddling back to shore, where she gratefully dragged the board onto firm sand, plonked her butt, and watched Archer strut his stuff.

The guy was seriously good—cresting waves, twisting and turning on his board with precision, looking like the poster boy for surfing that he was.

She could have watched him for hours, but a few minutes later he coasted into shore, picked up his board, tucked it under his arm and jogged towards her.

For some inexplicable reason she felt compelled to get up and run to meet him halfway. Last night when he'd comforted her might have been the catalyst, or maybe his admission on the beach earlier today, but whatever it was she felt she wanted to be close to him.

As he drew near the urge intensified, and when he smiled at her, with tiny rivulets of sea water running down that impossibly handsome face, her heart twisted like one of the fancy manoeuvres he'd pulled out there.

She wanted him.

With a desperation that clawed at all her well-formulated, highly logical reasons why she shouldn't, shredding them beyond repair.

'You're looking at me like I'm Red Riding Hood and you're the big bad wolf.' He laid the board down and sat beside her. 'My showy moves impress you?'

'*You* impress me,' she said, sucking in a deep breath and covering his hand with hers.

His questioning stare snagged hers, and with her heart pounding loud enough to drown out the breaking surf she leaned across and did what she should have had the guts to do earlier that morning.

She kissed him.

Archer had pulled some pretty fancy moves out there. Show-pony stunts: fins out, a sharp turn where the fins slide off the top of the wave; soul arch, arching his back to demonstrate his casual confidence; switch-foot, changing from right to left foot forward, and hang-ten, putting ten toes over the nose of his long board.

Usually when he hit the waves he surfed for himself, for the sheer pleasure it brought him. It was that enjoyment that gave him the edge in competitions, for he concentrated on fun and not his opponents.

Not today. Today he'd surfed to impress Callie.

By that lip-lock she'd just given him it had worked. And how.

If he'd known that was all it would take he would have hit the waves the first day they'd arrived.

'You're grinning like an idiot,' she said, nudging him with her elbow.

'It's not every day a guy gets a kiss like that for balancing on a few waves.'

She rolled her eyes. 'Give me a break. You get smooches from bikini babes every time you win a tournament.'

'Congratulatory kisses.' He traced her lower lip with his fingertip, exploring the contour, feeling the faintest wobble. 'Nothing compared to that lip-smacker you just planted on me.'

She blushed, but to her credit didn't look away. 'You wanted a date for the wedding. I'm just trying to make it look authentic.'

'How authentic do you want to get?' He puckered up in a ludicrous parody and she chuckled.

'How important is it for you to convince them I'm the real deal?'

His smile faltered as her innocent question hit unerringly close to home. 'Hold my hand, gaze adoringly into my eyes, smooch a little. Well, actually, a lot. That should do the trick.'

'So why would you need a date to your brother's wedding anyway?'

He'd been waiting for her to ask that for days, but she'd been so hell-bent on burying her nose in business and avoiding him that they hadn't strayed into personal territory. It looked as if last night had well and truly changed all that.

'Things with my folks are a little tense when I come home for flying visits. It's awkward.'

He waited for the inevitable *why* but she surprised him, tilting her head to one side as if studying him. 'I'm surprised a tough guy like you can't handle a little *awkward.*'

He should have known she wouldn't buy his trite answer. But how could he tell her the rest without having to answer a whole lot of other questions he'd rather left unsaid?

'It's easier this way.' He snagged her hand and pressed a kiss to her palm, enjoying the flare of heat in her eyes. 'And much more enjoyable with a date I actually like.'

Her nose crinkled adorably. 'You *like* me? What are you? In fifth grade?'

'You'll be pleased to know I'm a lot more experienced than I was in fifth grade,' he said, tugging on her hand until she almost straddled his lap. 'I like you, Callie. You know that. And I'd like nothing more than to spend the next few days showing you how much.'

He expected her to bolt again. To revert back to business mode. To resurrect the invisible wall she'd steadfastly maintained since they'd arrived.

Instead, she surprised him.

She captured his face between her hands and gently bridged the distance, whispering against the side of his mouth, 'Then what are we waiting for?'

Callie didn't want time to second guess her impulse.

She wanted Archer.

Now.

'Let's get cleaned up, grab some dinner, then head home—'

'No.' It almost sounded like a desperate yell, and she laughed to cover her nervousness. 'I—I want this to be like in Capri.'

His eyes widened at the implication.

He remembered. Remembered that hedonistic time in a sheltered alcove on a deserted beach. Remembered the frantic hands and straining mouths and incredible eroticism of it.

'You sure?'

'Never been surer of anything in my life.'

And then she promptly made a mockery of her brave declaration by stumbling as she tried to stand.

He steadied her, his gaze never leaving hers. 'Cal, do we need to talk about afterwards? Because nothing will change. Our lives are separate—'

'Since when did you talk so much?'

She silenced him with a kiss—a hot, open-mouthed kiss designed to distract and titillate and eradicate any lingering doubts they might harbour.

When they finally came up for air, he held her hand as if he'd never let go. 'There's a bunch of deserted dunes just over that hill.'

She liked how he didn't spell it out, how he left the option up to her with his silent challenge.

Tilting her head to meet his heated gaze, she tried her best sexy smile and hoped it didn't come out a grimace. 'Lead the way.'

After making a detour to the sheds, where they struggled out of their wetsuits and Archer snagged his wallet and a throw rug, they ran, their feet squeaking on the clean sand, their soft panting in rhythm with her pounding heart.

When they crested the hill and she saw the pristine dunes stretched out before them tears stung her eyes.

It was so beautiful. A perfect place to resurrect incredible memories and to create new ones.

They didn't speak as he led her by the hand to a secluded spot sheltered by an overhanging rock, laid out the rug, and knelt.

She'd never felt so worshipped as she did at that moment, with the guy she'd once had serious feelings for kneeling at her feet and staring up at her in blatant adoration.

When he tugged on her hand she joined him on the rug and in a flurry of whispered endearments, sensual caresses, and mind-blowing passion they came together.

Afterwards, as Archer cradled her in his arms and she stared at the seagulls wheeling overhead, Callie wondered one thing.

What the hell have I done?

CHAPTER SEVEN

'SHOULD'VE known you two bozos couldn't keep your big traps shut.'

Archer glared at Trav and Tom, who merely grinned and raised their beer bottles in his direction.

'What do you mean? This barbecue's in lieu of Trav's rehearsal dinner. You had to come.' Tom smirked and gave a less than subtle head-jerk in Callie's direction. 'And you couldn't leave your wedding date at home. That just wouldn't be right.'

Archer punched him on the arm. 'I had to tolerate Mum's interrogation on the phone for thirty minutes this arvo, and I've spent the last hour dodging her since we arrived, thanks to you.'

Tom raised his beer. 'You can thank me properly when she's presiding over *your* wedding.'

'Like hell,' Archer muttered, the thought of marriage making his chest burn like he'd scoffed a double-pepperoni pizza.

'It happens to the best of us, bro.' Trav nudged him and Archer frowned. 'You lot are a poor example to bachelors the world over.'

'Hey, *I'm* a bachelor.' Tom thrust his chest out and beat it with his fists like a gorilla and they laughed.

'With behaviour like that I'm not surprised,' Trav said,

pointing at a group of his fiancée's friends clustered around the chocolate fountain. 'Shelly has loads of nice single friends. Why don't you go chat up one of them?'

Tom shrugged, his nonchalance undermined by the way his fingers gripped his beer. 'Not interested.'

'Not every woman's like—'

'Trav, Shelly's calling you,' Archer said, earning a grateful glance from Tom.

'Think about it. Izzy needs a mum.'

Archer stiffened, expecting Tom to fire a broadside at Travis, but he merely muttered 'Punk' under his breath as Trav headed for his bride-to-be with the swagger of a young guy in love.

'At the risk of being bashed over the head with that bottle, maybe Trav's right.'

As expected, Tom bristled. 'Izzy and I are doing just fine.'

'I know you are, mate, but she's growing up.'

He glanced at his niece, her blonde pigtails streaming behind her as she raced across the lawn in pursuit of a rabbit. 'She's six going on sixty, and one day soon you'll find her asking a bunch of questions you'd rather not answer.'

To his surprise, Tom seemed to deflate before his eyes. 'She's an amazing kid.' He dragged a hand across his eyes, blinking as if he'd just woken up. 'She's my world.'

'Then maybe you should think about joining the land of the living again?' Archer hoped to lighten the sombre mood. 'When's the last time you had a date anyway?'

Old hurts darkened Tom's mood and his usually jovial brother frowned. Archer felt like a jerk for probing his wounds but Trav was right. Tom needed to start dating again—for his own sake as well as Izzy's.

Not that he had a right to butt in where his niece was concerned, considering his deliberate distancing over the years. But this visit was different. Seeing Callie interact with his family made him appreciate them in a whole new light. And made him feel like a first class jerk.

How long would he keep his own old hurts locked away inside where they festered? How long would he let wounded pride get in the way?

Tom's turbulent gaze focussed on his daughter as he placed his bottle on a nearby table and folded his arms. 'You ever wish you had a different life?'

Never. Discounting the hash of a relationship he now had with his family.

Archer loved his life: the freedom, the buzz, the adrenalin. He liked being his own boss, and valued his independence as much as his trophies. Though he'd be lying if he didn't admit to wondering more and more these days why he was so hell-bent on the single life.

At the start it had been about striving for success and not needing ties to hamper him. Emotional ties that ended up causing pain.

His family might not know it, but in their decision to ostracise him from his dad's illness and not trust him enough to cope they'd solidified his life choices.

Better for him not to connect emotionally with anyone, to enjoy his lack of responsibility and savour the single life. No strings attached; a motto that had served him well over the years.

Callie's laughter floated on the breeze and something in his gut clenched.

No, he didn't regret a thing, but for a moment he wondered how different his life would have been if he'd put his trust issues aside and taken a risk on their relationship.

'No use wondering about maybes, mate. All we can do is make the best of what we've got.'

Pensive, Tom nodded. 'I don't regret marrying Tracy for

the sake of Izzy, that's for sure. But sticking around here with its same-old, same-old has its moments.'

Tom wouldn't get any arguments from him. The monotony of living in the small town he'd grown up in would've driven him nuts.

'What about surfing?'

Tom's frown deepened. 'What about it?'

'Do you resent not going pro?'

'Hell, no.' Tom guffawed. 'I was never as driven as you, squirt. No way would I have spent years traipsing the world chasing the next big wave.'

'It was all you talked about growing up. I think it's half the reason I wanted to go pro—because you did.'

Tom shook his head. 'You always wanted it more than me. I couldn't hack all the training and moving around.'

'But I thought…'

'What?'

'That you gave it all up when Trace deliberately got pregnant. That she trapped you and you hated it and that's what eventually led to the marriage falling apart.'

Tom slapped him on the back. 'Not that it matters now, but to set the record straight—yeah, Tracy fell pregnant on purpose, but she didn't trap me. I didn't have to propose. I wanted to, because I was young and dumb and idealistic.'

He glanced towards their folks, toasting each other with champagne at a quiet table at the rear of the marquee, oblivious to the family bedlam around them. 'I guess I secretly wanted what they had.'

A familiar sadness enveloped Archer when he glanced at his folks. The Fletts had always been a close family, and his folks seemed more devoted now, following the health scare that had so shocked him when he'd eventually found out.

He envied them that closeness. It was like standing on the outside looking in at an exclusive club.

Tom's mouth twisted into a wry smile. 'I'd give an arm and a leg to have a relationship like that. A woman who adores me, who's content to be with me and doesn't need all the fancy trappings of a big city.'

Liking the fragile bond of reconnecting with Tom on a deeper level than mock-wrestling, Archer delved further. 'Is that why Tracy left? Because she wanted the high life?'

''Course. Once she had Izzy it was all she talked about. I wanted a future that focussed on building a stable environment for our child to grow in, and she couldn't leave fast enough.'

Archer rubbed the back of his neck, wondering if Santa would make an appearance to dispel any other myths he'd once believed in.

'Wow, I didn't know.'

'Because some things are best left unsaid. Besides, I don't want Iz hearing bad stuff about her mum, just in case Trace grows a conscience one day and wants to see her daughter.'

'Where is she?'

'Sydney, last I heard but who knows? She sends the obligatory birthday and Christmas gifts. That's about it.'

While Tom's tone didn't hold an ounce of censure, guilt niggled at Archer.

Was that how the Fletts talked about *him* when he wasn't around? Saying that he should *grow a conscience* rather than sending *obligatory* birthday gifts and making an *obligatory* Christmas visit during which he couldn't wait to escape back to his life?

Considering how he'd withdrawn from them, he couldn't blame them.

He *wanted* to forgive and move on.

He *wanted* to shelve his pride and bring the whole thing out into the open.

But every single time he wanted to broach the painful subject of how he'd felt at being shut out, and how their rebuttal of his overture had hurt, one image stuck in his mind.

His dad, elbows braced on his precious piano, head in his hands, crying. Big, brusque Frank Flett never cried, and to see his father so broken had left a lasting legacy.

It had been just after they'd finally told him the truth— a year after his dad had been given the all-clear. Twelve freaking months, on top of the six months Frank had battled the disease that could have claimed his life, when his family had shut him out because they didn't want to distract him, or thought he couldn't handle it, or some such rot.

He'd been livid, and seeing his father's tears had reinforced what they thought of him as nothing else could.

If his dad could still cry when he was cancer-free, how bad must it have been during the long battle of surgery, chemo and the rest?

A battle *he'd* been excluded from because they'd deemed him not responsible enough to handle it.

His hands unconsciously clenched into fists and he inhaled, forcing himself to calm down before any of his bitterness spilled out.

'What's wrong?' Tom's perceptive stare bored into him and he glanced away.

'Nothing.'

'Like hell.' Tom paused, made an exasperated sound. 'Is that why you keep running? Because you think I got trapped, gave up a dream, and you don't want the same to happen to you?'

Archer's tension eased as he saw Callie strolling towards the bar, her pale lemon floral dress swishing around her calves, making her look ethereal and pretty and all too ravishing.

What could he say?

The truth?

That he didn't dare trust an incredible woman like Callie? That even now, after the incredible reconnection they'd shared last night, first at the beach and later at his house, he was absolutely terrified of giving in to the feelings she evoked?

He settled for a partial truth. 'You know I wanted out of Torquay, and surfing was my ticket out. No harm in following your dreams.'

'Unless it interferes with what you really want.'

Archer glared at his brother, not liking the direction this conversation was taking.

'How would you know what I really want?'

'Because I see the way you look at Callie.'

He hated Tom's condescending smirk as much as his homing in on his innermost fears.

'And I'd hate to see you throw away a chance at real happiness because you're stuck on some warped idea that being in a relationship means giving up your freedom.'

That was not the only thing being in a relationship meant. Reliance, trust, love, they were all a part of it too, and those were the things or, more to the point, the loss of those things that ensured he'd never let Callie get too close.

She'd almost made him slip once before.

Not this time.

'You've been watching too many chick-flicks after Izzy's in bed,' he said, wanting to wipe the infuriating, know-all expression off Tom's face. 'I *like* my life. I'm doing what I want to do, so lay off.'

'Truth hurts, huh?'

Archer swore. 'How about you concentrate on getting your own love-life in order and leave me the hell alone?'

He stalked off a few paces. Not far enough to escape Tom's taunt.

'Who said anything about love?'

He strode faster. He might be able to outrun his brother's annoying chuckles, but he couldn't shake the insistent little voice in his head that focussed on that one little L-word and its disastrous implications.

Callie's head ached.

Bad enough she'd spent the last twenty-four hours over-analysing her impulsiveness in tumbling into a physical relationship with Archer—now she'd inadvertently joined the unofficial Archer Flett Fan Club.

Ever since she'd arrived at the party she'd been bombarded with glowing recommendations from every female family member. And the interrogation from the Flett females was truly frightening.

They wanted to know *everything*.

And she didn't know what to tell them. What could she say? That she'd handed Archer her heart eight years ago, he'd trampled it, and now she'd foolishly come back for more?

Uh-uh. So she'd glossed over her relationship with Archer as being old friends catching up while he was in Melbourne. Interestingly, Shelly had revealed what a refreshing change she was from Archer's usual dates, '*snobby, plastic, citified bimbos*', who wouldn't mingle let alone talk to his family.

She'd wanted to pry, but Archer's mum had shot Shelly a warning look and she'd clammed up. Not that Callie wanted to acknowledge the twinge of jealousy, but considering how warm and welcoming Archer's family had been towards *her*, she was surprised he'd bring that type of woman home.

That was another thing. His interaction with his family. Something was definitely *off*.

He'd been nervous about attending this party. She'd seen it back at his place, subtle signs that his usual confidence was rattled: pacing the balcony while she'd been getting ready, sculling caffeine drinks, absentmindedly changing TV channels without watching any show.

When she'd asked him about it he'd laughed it off, but she'd known there was more to it when he'd taken his sweet time getting out of the car when they'd arrived and then remained on the outskirts the entire party.

She'd seen him talking to his brothers, but beyond a perfunctory greeting for his parents he'd kept his distance from them.

Which begged the question *why*?

She'd ask later—add it to the million other questions buzzing around her brain. Questions she should have asked before falling in lust with him all over again.

One thing was for sure: Archer's family wanted him to stick around for a change. No way would she break the news to them that there was more chance of her winning the next surf pro classic than Archer Flett putting down roots.

He was a confirmed nomad, and in a way it added to his charm. His impulsiveness, his spontaneity, his live-for-the-moment attitude. What they'd done on the beach...the memory had her running a chilled glass across her forehead. It did little to cool the scorching images replaying like a naughty film.

Archer peeling off her swimsuit, exploring every inch of her body with strong, sure hands, kissing her everywhere...

'You can get arrested for looking like that.'

Archer's whisper fanned her ear, sending little pin-wheels of sensation ricocheting through her as his arm slid around her waist, anchoring her to him.

As if she'd want to run. Her surname wasn't Flett. More was the pity.

'Like what?'

He growled at her *faux* innocence. 'Like you've spent the day in bed and you can't wait to get back there.'

She glanced up at him from beneath her lashes. 'Who said anything about a bed? As I recall, the beach served us just fine—'

'Stop, you're killing me.'

His grip tightened as he swung her around, protecting her from prying eyes and backing her towards the rear of the marquee.

'Like you haven't been thinking about it,' she said, challenging him to open up a tad.

They hadn't talked much since the beach, and had fallen into a physical relationship as easily as they'd tumbled in Capri. It had suited her yesterday, not discussing much beyond the present. She'd been on a high, wallowing in the decadence of being in Archer's arms again.

But today reality had set in.

Considering their proximity, living together, it had been all too easy—almost inevitable—sliding back into a physical relationship with the underlying attraction still sizzling between them.

It shouldn't mean anything. Sadly for her it did.

Getting physical with Archer had thrust her right back to the same place she'd been eight years earlier: knowing there'd be an expiration date and not liking it.

She also didn't like being vulnerable to him, and that

was exactly what she'd made herself in opening herself to him again.

Incredibly foolish, considering Archer hadn't fundamentally changed. Footloose, fancy-free and loving it.

The situation reminded her of the many times she'd taken a chance on her dad, when he'd blown into her life, swept her off her feet with gifts and empty promises, only to forget her when he left.

It had been such a buzz being around him. But later the let-down and disappointment and devastation had sucked.

With Archer in Capri she'd made the mistake of masking her feelings, pretending a fling was no big deal. This time she wouldn't be so stupid.

At the start of this week they might have agreed that spending time together in Torquay was about work and being his date in exchange for the surf school campaign, but getting physical had changed the boundaries.

Their futures weren't intersecting, but this time she deserved more. She deserved answers.

Why had he really asked her to be his date for the wedding? How could he be so caring with her, especially about her mum, and shut down around his family?

What were his plans? Because from all accounts the guys at the surf school she'd spoken to had collectively mentioned that Archer would be around more often. What could that potentially mean for them?

Because she wouldn't let him walk away this time. Not without a fight.

She wasn't the same idealistic, naïve girl she'd been in Capri. Life was short—too short—and second chances were rare, so if she and Archer had a remote shot at making some kind of relationship work she'd take it.

She didn't want deep and meaningful, but something

casual and fun to lighten her days in the tough time ahead with her mum. She was all for that.

Ironic how she'd changed in a few days. She'd initially thought Archer wasn't a keeper, wasn't the kind of guy who'd support her when the going got tough.

Maybe he still wouldn't, but the more she saw him interact with his brothers, Izzy and the teenage surf crew, the more he held her and talked to her about her mum's illness and what he could do to raise awareness of her horrid disease, the more she realised she'd misjudged him.

He might have broken her heart eight years ago, but she'd changed. Why couldn't she believe he had too?

Only one way to find out.

Ask the hard questions.

Archer nuzzled her neck. 'I've been thinking of getting you naked again ever since we got here, but there are children present.'

Those questions she needed to ask were momentarily put on hold. 'Stop. People might see.'

'Let them,' he said, his lips trailing down her neck towards her collarbone, nipping along the way.

Her skin rippled with sensation as she arched towards him, wanting whatever he could give.

A low wolf-whistle signalled the arrival of company and Archer swore as they disentangled. 'If that's Tom I'm going to kill him,' he said as Callie readjusted her skewed dress straps.

'Sorry to interrupt, but we're doing speeches.' Travis grinned, not sorry in the least.

Archer shot him a death glare. 'Can't you leave that boring stuff until the wedding?'

'Why? Got better things to do?'

The corners of Archer's mouth curved up and Callie's

heart gave a little kick. She loved that half-smile, as if he was genuinely amused and loving life.

'Yeah, and if you had any sense you'd be doing the same thing rather than getting caught up in all this wedding nonsense.'

'Hey, why not add to the Christmas festivities with a rousing Flett shindig? Keeps the folks sweet, that's for sure.'

'It's a sad day when a Flett male turns into a romantic sap,' he said. An odd expression Callie couldn't fathom flitted across Archer's face as he released her waist to snag her hand.

'We'll be there in a sec,' he added.

A little frown creased Travis's brow but he merely nodded and walked away, leaving her the perfect opportunity to discover what it was about his family that made Archer tense up.

'I've ordered a whole lot of online gift cards for your family for Christmas. Think that'll be okay?'

'Fine,' he said. But clearly it wasn't. That little exchange with his brother had left Archer edgy and reticent and standoffish.

She preferred him laid-back and happy, but she wanted answers and there was only one way to get them.

'Why do you do that?'

He shot her a confused glance. 'What?'

'Close off around your family.'

His brow instantly furrowed. 'That's bull—'

'Is it?'

His lips compressed as he stared at his parents, in deep conversation with Tom on the other side of the marquee.

When he didn't answer, she continued. 'When your brothers showed up at your house and I walked into the kitchen I could feel the tension. Since then you've spent

all your time either working or surfing and haven't visited your folks.'

The slash between his brows deepened.

'And tonight, rocking up to this party seems like the
last thing you wanted to do.' She blew out a long breath.
He was still here, listening. She took it as a good sign.
'Your family can't speak highly enough of you, so I don't
get it. Maybe—'

'Maybe you should butt out.'

Hurt slashed her hopes. Hope he'd changed, hope he'd
trust her with the truth, hope they had a future.

She tugged on her hand, but rather than releasing it
as she'd expected he held on tighter and swore under his
breath. When he finally looked at her, the pain in his eyes
made her breath catch.

'Sorry for snapping at you.' He gestured towards his
family with his free hand. 'None of this is your fault.'

'Want to talk about it?'

'Not really.'

But he did. She could see the turbulent conflict tearing
him up inside as his wild gaze swung between Tom, Trav,
his folks and Izzy.

It was as if he waged some great inner battle before his
stare softened, fixed on Izzy.

'I'm not around much any more. I feel like a stranger.'

He said it so softly she had to lean into him to hear, and
the underlying sadness in his reluctant admission tore at
her heart.

'My fault, not theirs,' he added, his hand gripping hers
as if he'd never let go. 'It's like once I hit the surf circuit I
didn't belong here any more.'

Silence stretched as she tried to come up with something to say that didn't sound trite.

'Your lives are so different. Maybe having less in common made you feel like that?'

'It's not that,' he said, his eyes bleak as he tore his gaze away from his family and refocussed on her. 'They kept something from me. It changed everything.'

Oh, heck. She could see it was big from his shattered expression. She'd wanted answers; she hadn't wanted to cause him this much pain.

'What happened?'

He sucked in a deep breath and blew it out in a long stream.

'Dad had prostate cancer. They didn't tell me for eighteen months.'

Stunned, she stared at him in disbelief. She couldn't comprehend the enormity of how betrayed she'd feel if her mum hadn't told her the truth about her disease. And in that moment she understood everything: Archer's discomfort around his family, his unwillingness to get too close.

'I'm so sorry,' she said, pulling him in for a comforting hug that didn't convey half of what she wanted to say.

'It sucked.' He disengaged, the slight catch in his voice underscoring his vulnerability. 'Apparently he was diagnosed around the time I first started making a name for myself on the pro circuit. A couple of years before we first met.'

His gaze swung back to his family.

'They didn't want to burden me with something I could do little about. They waited to tell me once he'd got the all-clear so I would follow my dream.' He dragged a hand through his hair. 'Damn it, do you have any idea how shallow that makes me sound?'

Wishing she could do something to ease his pain, she captured his chin and made him look at her.

'Don't judge them too harshly. I've been where they are,

sitting around helpless and frustrated, waiting for results. It's a relentless, mundane task that eats away at you, and there isn't one damn thing you can do about any of it.' She released him, shaken by the vehemence of her response. 'I know how hurt you must've been at being shut out, but did you stop to think they did it because they love you?'

Confusion clouded his eyes and she continued. 'You told me in Capri that all you'd ever wanted growing up was to be the best surfer in the world. You said that every night you poured into getting your degree part-time was because you wanted to *be* something. Something beyond a local Torquay guy with big dreams and little else.'

She grabbed his arms and gave him a little shake. 'You wanted it so badly I envied you that certainty of what you wanted and how far you'd go to get it. If I picked up on that in a week, don't you think your family knew how much your dream meant to you?'

He opened his mouth to respond and she placed a fingertip under his chin and gently closed it. 'Think about this. If you'd known and given up everything to be with your dad, would you have ended up resenting your family because of it?'

''Course not. I should've been here, supporting them.'

She shook her head. 'You're telling me the independent, driven, determined guy I know would've been happy giving up his dream to stay in Torquay?'

His frown was back. 'It was my decision to make, and they didn't give me a choice.'

His hurt was audible and she cupped his cheek. 'They love you, Arch, and your dad's fine. That's all that matters. Don't waste time on regrets, because life's too short.'

She saw the moment some of his load eased. His confusion cleared and clarity shone through.

'Is that why you gave me a second chance?'

His question came out of left field and stunned her a little. Of course her 'seize the day' mentality had a lot to do with her mum's illness and her approach to life, but him being intuitive enough to pick up on it—and call her on it—really surprised her.

He slid his arms around her waist and rested his forehead against hers. 'I'm sorry for the way things ended.'

Her heart stalled. There was so much she wanted to say, so much more she wanted to ask, but she'd made great inroads in getting him to open up about his family—who were now gathering for speeches and sending curious glances their way. The rest would have to wait until later.

'Me too,' she said, easing away, needing to lighten the mood before she started bawling. 'You know, the faster we get the speeches over with, the faster we can get out of here.'

'I like the way you think,' he said, dropping a quick kiss on her lips.

CHAPTER EIGHT

ARCHER'S guts griped the way they had the time he'd eaten too many jalapeños in Mexico. Sadly, what ailed him this time wouldn't be fixed with a dose of alka selzer.

This was what opening up did to a guy: it made him feel as if he'd be sick at any moment.

How the hell had Callie done that? Wormed some of the truth out of him? He hadn't told anyone about his dad's illness for fear it would paint him in a bad light. Not that he'd been deliberately uncaring. He just hadn't been given the chance to care.

But having Callie articulate his family's possible motivation in keeping such a momentous thing from him had gone some way to assuaging the pain.

Maybe it was time to swallow his damn pride and try to start building a few bridges again?

'Come with me.' His grip tightened on Callie's hand, and as she smiled up at him a new pang twisted his gut.

This one had nothing to do with old regrets and everything to do with a new realisation.

That Callie meant more to him than he'd like to admit.

'Sure. Though if I have to listen to one more anecdote about you guys terrorising Torquay by running around naked as kids I'm bailing.'

'I don't hear you complaining about seeing me naked

now,' he said, his low voice making her eyes widen. The molten depths urged him to head home with her right this very minute, bridges be damned.

'I'm assuming we're heading over to your family to say goodbye?'

He grinned at her cool delivery, spoiled by her healthy blush.

'You assume right.' He ducked down to whisper in her ear. 'The sooner I get you naked the better.'

Her blush intensified and he was chuckling, as Izzy bowled up to him and careened into his legs, almost up-ending both of them.

'Hey, Iz, where's the fire?'

'You're leaving,' she said, hanging off his leg in a similar way he'd seen her do to her dad. 'And I don't want you to go.'

Hell.

Intuitive as usual, Callie squeezed his hand and released it so he could squat down to Izzy's level. She transferred her death grip from his leg to his arm.

'I'm not going far, Iz, just up the road.'

Her blue eyes narrowed, pinning him with the retribution of a child he'd let down too many times in the past. 'You sure you're coming to the wedding on Christmas Eve and everything?'

'I'm sure.'

Her wariness didn't ease, and he half expected her to give him a kick in the shins for all those times he'd side-stepped her too-astute questions about his early departure.

'Okay, then,' she said, but she didn't let go, and as she stared at him with wide-eyed suspicion it hit him.

Izzy didn't believe him.

And that more than anything Callie had said or his family could say got through to him. He needed to stop thinking about making amends and actually start doing something about it.

'Hey, Iz, I know things are kinda busy around here, with everyone getting ready for Uncle Trav's wedding, but if it's okay with your dad why don't I take you surfing tomorrow?'

She stared at him in disbelief for a good five seconds before an ear-splitting grin indicated he'd done the right thing.

With a loud screech that had every guest in the place looking their way, she released him and ran towards Tom, about six feet away, yelling loud enough to be heard in Melbourne. 'Uncle Arch is taking me surfing! Yay, yay, *yay*!'

His family stared at him in unison.

Tom's warning glare spoke volumes: *You'd better not let my kid down this time.*

Trav was giving him a thumbs-up of encouragement.

His mum's soft smile was warm and appreciative and hopeful.

His dad gave a brief nod of approval before he glanced away, unable to look him in the eye as usual.

Well, he'd *make* Frank Flett look him in the eye before he left this time. If the surf school didn't show his dad he was worthy and responsible he'd face this situation head-on regardless.

Callie's pep talk had got him thinking. He'd spent too many years being an outcast in his own family—his choosing. Time to discover the truth about what had happened during his dad's illness, and why they hadn't deemed him fit to know at the time.

And he had Callie to thank for giving him the push he needed.

'Thanks.' He caressed her cheek with his fingertips, a

fleeting gesture he hoped conveyed even half of what he was thinking.

'For what?'

'Everything,' he said, pulling her in for a quick hug to the sound of embarrassing applause from his family.

She laughed as they disengaged, and as he took in her flushed cheeks and sparkling eyes and smiling mouth he realised how much he'd given up in walking away from her all those years ago.

And he'd end up doing it again.

He didn't want to lose her, but he didn't trust himself to make her happy. He'd analysed it at length: if his family didn't trust him when the going got rough, was it *him*?

Was it because he didn't inspire trust in people? And if his own family didn't trust him, how could he connect emotionally with a woman like Callie?

Where did that leave them?

Damned if he knew.

While Izzy alternated between dancing around Tom and tearing towards him, he grabbed Callie's hand and tugged her towards his family.

He made arrangements with Tom to pick up Izzy in the morning, slapped Trav on the back and hugged his mum.

When it came to Frank, the inevitable questions bubbled to the forefront of his mind.

Why didn't you tell me, Dad?

Why didn't you let me be there for you?

Why did you trust the others and not me?

He didn't ask. Now wasn't the time. But before he left this trip he'd discover the truth behind all the pain.

They stood there, self-conscious and ill at ease. Archer wanted to say so much, yet he was plagued by the same discomfort that inevitably occurred around his dad these days. When Frank tried a tentative grin Archer shook his hand and mumbled something about seeing him at the wedding. He wanted answers, but right now he was plain exhausted.

This emotional re-bonding took it out of a guy, and hot on the heels of his realisation that he didn't want to lose Callie…well, Archer knew he had some serious thinking to do.

When Archer had invited Izzy to surf he'd envisaged the two of them having a little uncle-niece bonding time.

What he *hadn't* imagined was the entire Flett clan descending on the beach for an impromptu picnic. Izzy loved the attention and the mayhem and the laughter. Him—not so much.

As he watched Trav elbow their dad and share a laugh with him on the foreshore, regret strengthened his resolve to put the past behind him and move on.

Regret that he'd missed out on being there for his dad when he'd needed him most.

Regret that he'd missed out on so much with his family because of his deliberate withdrawal.

Regret that he hadn't confronted the issue sooner because of his damned pride.

'Hey, you're not watching me!' Izzy's yell refocussed his attention on where it should be: refining her pop up technique.

'I am now, squirt.'

As she sprang from her knees to a standing position, arms stretched out sideways, her grin wide and proud, some of his residual tension whenever his family were around eased.

He'd wasted enough time hanging onto old hurts, and he had missed out on spending time with Izzy as a result.

No more.

'You're a natural,' he said, sweeping her into his arms and tickling her until she squealed.

'I wanna go in the water,' she said, grabbing both his ears and twisting until he released her.

Rubbing them, he tried to frown and failed, his mouth twitching with suppressed laughter instead. 'Ow, Iz, that hurt.'

'Wuss,' she said, poking out her tongue, mischief sparking in blue eyes the colour of the ocean behind her.

'That's it. Lesson's over.'

She giggled and ran into the shallows, kicking water at him as he followed. They dodged and weaved and splashed until he tackled her, scooped her in his arms and made for deeper water.

'My daddy will get cross at you for taking me out so far.' She pouted, but there was no denying the mischievous twinkle in her eyes or mistaking the devious machinations of an intelligent, conniving child who'd say anything to avoid a good old-fashioned dunking.

'Your daddy's laughing as hard as Nan and Pop,' he said, laughing when she glanced towards shore and saw he spoke the truth.

'Put me down,' she said, pummelling his shoulders, so he obliged, chuckling as a wave swamped them and Iz resurfaced, a wide-eyed, bedraggled imp with a grin as wide as the stretch of beach.

Archer lost track of how long they frolicked in the waves—duck-diving, playing tag—and he didn't care. The longer he stayed out here with Izzy, in the one place he felt truly at home, the easier it became to let go of the past.

He'd recaptured some of the magic with his niece and he'd be damned if he lost it again.

Now if only he could do the same with his dad.

'I'm hungry,' Izzy said, flinging her arms around his neck and hanging on tight. 'And thirsty.'

'Okay, kiddo, let's go attack that mountain of food your nan brought along.'

As he waded into shore with Izzy in his arms and strode towards his family their collective expressions gave him hope for the future. Approval, warmth, relief and optimism—the latter on his dad's weather-lined face as admiration lit his smile.

Yeah, it was definitely time to put the past behind him, and he owed it all to Callie.

As if on cue she popped out from the main office of the surf school, where she'd been putting a few finishing touches to the website.

He saw her glance towards his family, sprawled across a picnic blanket on the sand in casual unanimity, and back to him, as if unsure whether to join them or not.

Later. For now he had to thank her.

He lowered Izzy until her feet hit sand, savouring her hesitation to let him go. 'Save me a Vegemite sandwich, kiddo, I'll be there in a sec.'

'But I get the last brownie,' she flung over her shoulder, already racing towards the Fletts, where she flung herself into Tom's arms.

Archer had never envisaged himself settling down, let alone having kids, but watching his brother and niece rub noses in an affectionate greeting he damn well wanted what they had.

'You did a good thing today.'

Callie touched his arm, and the immediate lick of heat made him wish he could drag her back to their sand dune for a repeat performance of that time earlier in the week.

'What? Take my niece surfing?' He shook his head. 'I should've done it a long time ago.'

'It's never too late,' she said, and the barely audible quiver in her voice reminded him that for her, for her mum, one day it *would* be too late.

'Thanks.' He rested his hands on her waist, enjoying the way they seemed to belong there.

'For?'

'For giving me the kick up the ass I needed.'

Her gaze darted towards his family and a small, satisfied smile curved her lips. 'It's hard when you're too close to a situation. Sometimes all it takes is a little objectivity to help clear through the fluff.'

He chuckled. 'The fluff?'

Her gaze met his and it was as if he'd been dumped beneath a massive wave and couldn't catch his breath.

'The extra stuff that weighs us down and clouds our vision and makes us go a little crazy.'

She was something else.

Her beauty, her warmth, her wisdom.

And he'd let her go.

'I think I had some of that fluff clouding my judgement in Capri.'

Understanding sparked in her eyes and she opened her mouth to respond just as Izzy bowled into them like an out-of-control dervish.

'I've saved a sandwich for you, Uncle Arch. Come and get it.'

'Now, how can you refuse an offer like that?' Callie said as she ruffled Izzy's damp curls.

Izzy's nose crinkled in consternation. 'I don't think there's any more Vegemite ones for you, Callie, but I reckon you can have a piece of my fairy bread.'

'Sugar sprinkles? My favourite.' Callie slipped out of his grasp to hold Izzy's hand, but he snagged her arm before she could leave.

'You're amazing.'

He ducked down for a swift kiss, which resulted in a blush from Callie, an excited whoop from Izzy, and cheers from his family.

Yeah, he definitely had some talking to do later—with his dad and with Callie.

Christmas this year wasn't looking so bad after all.

'This place is awesome, dude.' Trav slapped Archer on the back as they entered the supply store at the end of the tour.

He'd been hyped, taking his family around the surf school while Callie entertained Izzy—who was demanding sandcastles—on the beach.

The Fletts' opinion of this place mattered.

He wanted them to like it. He wanted them to tell him he'd done good. Most of all he wanted them to realise he had a lot to give and was a guy of substance—not the flake they'd wrongly presumed.

'Great job, bro.' Tom shook his hand. 'Torquay needs something like this, a place where the kids can hang out.'

'Yeah, that's what I thought.'

They shared a conspiratorial smile, remembering their own tearaway teenage days and some of the mischief bored kids could get up to at the beach.

'I'm so proud of you, son.' His mum enveloped him in a squishy hug, the familiar lavender and fresh bread scent clinging to her so reminiscent of his childhood he felt choked up.

'Thanks, Mum.'

He hugged her tight, saddened by how much he'd missed over the years through the choices he'd made. Distancing himself from his family had probably hurt them, but he'd been the one to suffer the most.

They'd had each other.

He'd had no one.

He planned on changing all that.

When he released his mum, she moved over to the doorway, where Tom and Trav were deep in conversation. It gave Archer the opportunity to seek out his dad, who'd been hanging back during the tour.

While his brothers' and mother's opinion meant everything to him, it was Frank's he prized most.

Over the years they'd fallen into a pattern of mutual gruffness and avoidance that seemed impossible to breach.

Every time he made the slightest effort to reconnect his dad would brush it off as unnecessary in his usual jovial way. And Archer would let him. He never pushed the issue, his pride reiterating that there was only so far he could extend the olive branch and it was up to his dad to grab it.

Frank never had, and he hated the distance between them. He'd once idolised his dad. He'd always reckoned him, Tom and Trav had been super-lucky, having a hands-on dad who took them fishing and camping and hiking. Frank had attended every one of their footy matches, had never missed a training session either.

It made what had happened later all the harder to accept, and made Archer doubt himself as nothing else could.

Tired of second-guessing himself, and buoyed by the shove in the right direction Callie had given him, he had every intention of ensuring the gap between them wasn't irredeemable this time.

'What do you think, Dad?'

He hated having to ask, wished Frank had volunteered some faint praise without prompting, for it signalled that the divide between them was bigger than he'd anticipated.

'Good for Torquay.' Frank glanced around, stuck his hands in his pockets, shuffled his feet as if he couldn't wait to escape. 'Though it's a bit rough putting your name to something around these parts when you're going to be AWOL all the time.'

His dad's aloofness stung, but not as much as the barb behind his words. Frank hadn't acknowledged the good thing he'd done in setting up the school; he'd said it was good for the town.

As for the dig about him being away all the time, it might be true, but why couldn't his dad admit he was proud of him, rather than chastising him for having a school in his name?

'I may be around more often,' Archer said, making it sound blasé when in fact he was hanging on his dad's response.

Frank turned away, but not before he'd seen the scepticism twisting his mouth. 'Uh-huh.'

How two little syllables could hold so much doubt he'd never know.

Archer swallowed his disappointment. His pride in showing his family around and his hope for the future was shattered by his dad's continued standoffishness.

If Frank didn't get why he'd done this, couldn't bring himself to offer one word of positive encouragement, why the hell should he keep busting a gut trying to build bridges between them?

His pride might have kept him from being truly a part of this family all these years, but they'd wronged him first. Was that a childish way to look at it? Yeah, but as years' worth of hurt bubbled up from deep within it obliterated his intention to heal the rift between them.

'Why, Dad?'

Frank stiffened. 'Why what?'

Disgusted, Archer shook his head. 'You know what.'

'Frank, come take a look at this.'

Archer glanced at his mum. Her worried expression was

a dead giveaway that she'd sensed tension and was trying to avoid a messy confrontation.

Uncertain, Frank hesitated.

With disappointment warring with his bitterness, Archer said, 'Go.'

Which was exactly what he intended to do on Christmas Day, as planned.

Go back to his life, far from Torquay and the ghosts of the past haunting him.

'Come back to bed.'

Archer slid his arms around Callie from behind, resting his chin on her head.

'Just let me finish this.' She'd like nothing better than to slip back into his arms, but she had less than a day to get this website done and she didn't want to leave any loose ends.

Once Archer left she wanted a clean break. No contact.

It might be idealistic to hope for a stress-free resumption of their previous working relationship, where they e-mailed each other as needed, but she had a feeling Archer wouldn't mind.

Since Izzy's surf lesson and the impromptu Flett picnic at the beach this morning he'd withdrawn. Nothing overt, but she could tell.

She'd been here before.

In Capri it had been that silly joke she'd made about proposals in the Blue Grotto. Now she had no idea what had prompted his emotional shutdown.

From what she'd seen this morning he'd been closer to his family than he had all week. He'd been demonstrative and open and carefree—in his element.

Something must have happened during the tour of the surf school, because when they'd met up afterwards the tension between him and his dad had been so thick she was surprised it hadn't clouded the sky.

And he refused to discuss what was happening on Christmas Day with his family, despite her subtle prompting this afternoon. She had plans of her own to make, and the least he could do was let her in on what the heck was going on.

The Christmas holidays might not be a big deal for him, considering he lived his life on the road, but his youngest brother was getting married, for goodness' sake—surely this Christmas would be different?

'We've got all tomorrow morning to work on the website.' He ducked down beside her and kissed her cheek. 'Now's the time to play hooky.'

'Won't you have to do last-minute Christmas stuff before the wedding tomorrow night?'

Shadows darkened his eyes to indigo. 'Not really. Like you, I do all my shopping online, so stuff will get delivered direct to the family tomorrow.'

Knowing she was treading a hazardous path, she pushed away from the laptop and swivelled to face him.

'Don't you do other stuff?'

'Like?'

'Help your mum chop veggies for the roast on Christmas Day? Set the table? Fill stockings? That kind of thing?'

He stared at her as if she'd suggested he dress up as Santa and prance around Torquay lugging a sack for the day.

'I don't do that stuff.'

'Why?'

A part of her was dying to know, while the realistic part knew he'd never divulge the truth in a million years.

Guys like him didn't share deep, dark truths. They hid them away beneath a veneer of charm and practised wit.

She should know. Her dad had been the same.

A quick smile and a clever quip for everybody. Loving the world, but not staying put in one place long enough to form any real emotional attachments to anyone.

Including his own daughter.

She'd thought Archer was like that too until she'd seen the way he'd connected with those teenagers on the beach. And Izzy.

He genuinely cared about people, willingly gave of his time expecting nothing in return. That generosity came from within. It wasn't something you could fake; kids—especially teenagers—picked up on that kind of thing. She had with her dad.

Seeing that side of Archer, giving himself freely to those teens on the beach, had opened her eyes to his deeper facets—the ones he kept hidden. And it had made it pretty darn impossible to resist him.

Even with his complicated family history, why didn't he want to show that side of himself to *them*?

'I'm not around enough to warrant that kind of involvement in the rituals,' he said.

His jaw was clenched so hard she was surprised she couldn't hear his teeth grind.

'I fly in each year, stay a few days, then I'm outta here. Why disrupt their routine?'

'Maybe because they want you to?' She kept pushing, her previously undiscovered sadistic side wanting to prod an obvious wound. 'I know it's tough on you, after what you told me at the party, but your family light up when you're around.'

His sceptical glare indicated that he didn't believe her for a second. 'Prodigal son syndrome.'

She touched him on the arm. 'Why do you do that? Pretend your family isn't important to you?'

'That's bull.' He leaped to his feet as if she'd electrocuted him. 'They know how I feel about them.'

'Do they?'

She stood, wanting to see his reaction when she continued peppering him with bombshells. 'From what I've seen, Travis hangs on your every word, Tom looks out for you, and your folks think you walk on water rather than surf it.'

She reached for him, but he stepped away on the pretext of shutting a window, when in fact he was shutting her out.

'It's like they're vying for your attention and you don't want any of it.'

A tiny vein pulsed just below his ear, in the spot she loved to kiss. By his formidable glower, kissing was the last thing on his mind.

'You've met my family only a few times. A few more than any other woman I've known. What gives you the right to judge when you don't know them?'

Or me. The words hung unsaid between them and she resisted the urge to rub her chest where his barb had hit.

Because it was true.

She didn't really know him.

They'd connected for a brief seven days in Capri, but that had been mostly physical—as articulated by the man himself when he'd walked away.

As for their time together here… She'd fallen into the old trap of believing physical closeness implied intimacy, when in fact Archer didn't want to share anything with her. Not the stuff that mattered.

She wanted him to open up to her about what had happened earlier today to make him retreat—wanted him to trust her enough to do it. She'd thought they'd made major inroads in their developing relationship when he'd divulged the truth about his family at the party.

She'd been wrong.

For all she knew nothing had happened with his family during that tour this morning and he was deliberately closing off to *her*.

Maybe she'd been getting too close, and this was his way of cluing her in that come Christmas Day, when he dropped her home, they were finished.

Well, newsflash, surfer boy. She already knew they were over, but this time she wouldn't walk away with a whimper.

'So I'm supposed to be grateful you let me meet your family?' She slow clapped. 'Well done. You took the monumental step of letting a woman get closer than your bathrobe and a kiss on the cheek on her way out the next morning.'

Stricken, he paled, staring at her as if she'd morphed into a monster, and she knew she'd gone too far.

He was so infuriating, standing there in his emotional cocoon, holding everyone at bay when all they wanted to do was love him.

Her included.

Damn, she *loved* him.

Fine time to realise it. Her shock mirrored his.

'Sorry, that was way out of line. I'm just so mad at you for—'

'What, Callie? For walking away from you in Capri? For blackmailing you into being my date for the wedding? For sleeping with you again?' Anger radiated off him like a nuclear cloud. 'You've been mad at me since the day I stepped into your office.'

He jabbed a thumb at his chest. 'You've done such a great job of dumping home truths on *me*, why don't you take a look at yourself?' He took a step towards her, the air crackling with tension. 'Go on—admit it. You're still mad as hell for something that happened eight freaking years ago.'

She shook her head, close to tears. 'It's not that…'

He gripped her upper arms. 'Then tell me why you're so mad.'

She could have lied, could have made up some lame story, but that was what she'd done in Capri. Put on a brave face and lied when he made light of their week together.

Not this time.

'I'm mad at a lot of things, most of them beyond my control, but I'm mostly mad at myself.'

Confusion creased his brow and his grip on her arms eased now he was convinced this crazy woman wouldn't slug him. 'Why?'

'For being a hypocrite. For making light of what we share now, for calling it a fling and pretending I'm happy with it.'

Archer stiffened as she'd expected when she confronted him with the truth.

'I'm mad I let you walk away in Capri belittling what we'd had. I'm mad at you for not trusting me enough to tell me what's going on with you now. And most of all I'm mad as hell you're going to do the same thing this time around.'

Shock slashed his brow. 'I don't know what you want me to say.'

Saddened that even now, when she'd laid it on the line, he couldn't open up, she touched his cheek. 'That's the problem between us, isn't it?'

Fierce determination lit his eyes as he hauled her close. 'Callie, I don't know what you want me to say because I'm clueless here. I've never felt this way about anyone, but I can't change who I am.'

'I'm not asking you to change.'

Though inadvertently she was, and that wasn't fair. She didn't want Archer to give up his life.

She wanted him to love her the way she loved him.

And she couldn't make him love her. Just as she hadn't been able to make her dad love her.

That was when it hit her how alike the two really were. On the surface Archer appeared to be more giving of his time, but only with those not close to him. Why, she had no idea and she wouldn't waste time figuring it out.

How many years had her mum wasted trying to decipher her dad? How much time had Nora spent hoping Bruno would change, that he'd actually commit to something, even if it were only regular visits with his daughter, before being disappointed repeatedly?

She'd hated being second-best in her dad's affections, and no way in hell would she put herself through that with another guy who couldn't commit.

She'd finally told Archer the truth and, while he did care, he could never be the guy she wanted him to be.

So she had two choices.

End things now and spend the next day and the wedding being miserable.

Or make the most of their remaining time together.

Her mother's 'seize the day' attitude flashed through her mind.

'I'm not expecting anything from you.' She stepped into his personal space, almost treading on his toes, to whisper against his mouth. 'But it's Christmas Eve tomorrow and I have a few wishes I need to come true.'

Archer was too smart to buy her excuse completely, but she knew he wouldn't push it. She'd given him an out from the heavy, confrontational stuff and he'd take it. No doubt.

'Want to be my personal elf?' he said, a moment before he kissed her.

She loved this infuriating, emotionally repressed guy, and she'd be anything he wanted for the next twenty-four hours.

For come Christmas morning they'd be saying goodbye, and this time she didn't want to have any regrets.

CHAPTER NINE

ARCHER spent the morning at the surf school.

He'd always done his best thinking at Winki Pop, his go-to place when he'd been a kid. It was like home.

He owned property near Mavericks in Northern California, Pupukea on Oahu's north shore near the Pipeline, and Jeffreys Bay on the Eastern Cape of South Africa. Perfectly nice houses situated near the world's surfing hotspots—houses where he chilled at regular intervals.

But none brought him the peace of Winki Pop.

He'd surfed at dawn, eager to escape the house and Callie's all-seeing eyes.

She'd got close last night, too damn close, homing in on areas of his personal life strictly off-limits.

Hell, he could hardly go there himself.

He didn't get it. One minute he'd been coaxing her to come back to bed, the next she'd seen into his soul.

The thing was, she'd been right about some of it. He knew his family wanted more from him than he was willing to give. He saw it every time he came home—which was why he rarely did.

But this time he'd tried, damn it. Although he'd already made inroads with his brothers, his mum and Izzy, he'd finally done what he'd been yearning to do for years: tried to bridge the gap he'd created with his dad. But the way his dad had reacted at the surf school had demonstrated there was nothing he could say or do to mend metaphorical fences with him.

Because of that he'd been edgy since, and Callie had noticed. She hadn't pushed him and he'd appreciated it—until she'd blown up in his face last night.

When she'd admitted to considering their relationship more than a fling—then and now—he'd wanted to say so much, to lay it on the line: how he was feeling, what he was thinking. But with his dad's rejection fresh from the morning he hadn't been able to do it. Hadn't been able to take another chance with his jumbled, messed-up feelings.

Until he sorted out his options for the future, what would that mean for Callie? A casual relationship with benefits whenever he happened to be in town?

He doubted she'd put up with an arrangement like that, and he wouldn't want her to. She deserved more. More than he could give.

But for one infinitesimal moment, as he stared at the surfers bobbing like buoys on the ocean, he wondered what it would be like to have Callie on a permanent basis.

A woman to come home to.

A woman to love.

Shrugging off the terrifying thought, he resumed his final inspection.

As far as he could see the surf school was in tip top shape and ready for business.

Which was more than he could say for himself.

He was in lousy shape, and considering he not only had to face Christmas Eve but a Flett wedding too things could only go downhill.

Callie dressed with particular care.

She wanted to make this a night to remember.

She'd bought a knockout dress for the wedding from a local boutique expecting to show Archer what he was missing out on. Considering what they'd been up to the last few days, the strapless maroon chiffon cocktail dress with its flared skirt had become redundant.

Archer hadn't been missing out on anything.

Except the one thing she could never give him.

Her heart.

The realisation that she loved him shouldn't have come as any great surprise. She'd fallen hard during their week in Capri all those years ago—had only been saved from pining by her mum's diagnosis. But this time around it had hit her harder, and the constant slightly breathless feeling she had when he was near was beyond annoying.

She knew the score: there'd be no romantic proposals under the mistletoe for her this Christmas.

They were leaving first thing in the morning, apparently. Considering how his family had shut him out during his father's cancer battle she shouldn't be surprised he didn't want to spend Christmas Day with them.

She understood what it felt like when family let you down. She'd put up with it from her dad for too long, until she'd wised up and learned to expect nothing from the selfish, self-absorbed guy who valued his carefree lifestyle more than his only kid.

But from what she'd seen the Fletts were a close-knit, loving bunch. His parents had been married for yonks and still held hands, his youngest brother believed enough in romance to get married on Christmas Eve, and even Tom, who should be disillusioned after his wife had run off after less than twelve months of marriage, was keen to settle down again, according to Travis.

But, despite professing a wish to build bridges with his folks, Archer was still refusing to commit to them.

And her.

Foolish to think that way. Once he'd crept under her guard again and they'd fallen into a physical relationship she'd gone into it with her eyes wide open. In it for a short, good time, not a long time. A self-indulgent fling filled with amazing memories to sustain her through the tough times ahead.

In that respect getting involved with Archer again had exceeded her expectations. Every kiss, every touch, every whispered endearment had been imprinted on her brain to resurrect on a cold winter's night, when she was huddled over her computer working at midnight with a cooling coffee and a bowl of chocolate almonds for company.

Archer had been attentive, charming and altogether gorgeous over the last few days. Little wonder she'd fallen in love.

Her diaphragm gave a little spasm and she dragged in a deep breath and rubbed under her ribs. It didn't ease the stitch that grabbed her every time she associated the words 'love' and 'Archer' in the same thought.

She might be a realist, but the thought of spending the evening at a romantic wedding, the night in his arms and waking up together on Christmas morning made her want to bawl.

She had every intention to farewell him tomorrow, but it wouldn't be easy. Now she finally understood why her mum had secretly pined for Bruno's love all those years ago. *'We always want what we can't have,'* Nora had once said, in relation to Callie's pony request one Christmas, but by the tears in Nora's eyes Callie had known there was more to it.

Nora had led a full life, the epitome of a single mum who was loving it, but as a child Callie remembered hearing muffled sobs late at night, and seeing the way Nora lit up when Bruno returned home for a rare visit.

Callie empathised with her mum, but she didn't want to be that person. She didn't want to cry over lost love. She wanted to remember the good times and celebrate the second chance she'd had with Archer—even if it ended in tears like the first.

Snatching a tissue from the dresser, she dabbed under her eyes, absorbing the seepage. No way would she cry. Archer would be knocking on her bedroom door any moment and she wanted to wow him—not send him back to the surf school where he'd hidden out all day.

On the pretext of work, of course. A final inspection or some such guff. But she knew better.

He'd opened up a little last night and then emotionally closed down a lot. To the point where, when she'd shut down the program she'd been working on and backed up her work, he'd been asleep when she'd returned to bed. Or pretended to be.

She'd been too drained to care, but when she'd woken this morning to find a terse note and no Archer she'd had her answer to any silent questions she might have been contemplating.

Questions like had the last few days meant anything to him beyond a fling?

Did he feel their connection on a deeper level?

Would he walk away again without a backward glance?

Pointless questions, really, for even if he came up with the answers she wanted to hear it wouldn't change a thing. Her life was in Melbourne for the foreseeable future; his was traipsing the world. The closest they'd be was in cyber-space, where she'd contact him on a need-to-know basis. End of story.

A loud rap sounded on her door and she blinked rapidly, ensuring her eyes were sheen-free.

'Be right there.'

The incongruity of the situation struck her. They'd been intimate, this was *his* house, and yet he wouldn't open the door to her room.

Yeah, the barriers were already up, and the sooner she got used to it the better.

Attending this wedding, pretending she was happy, would be tough. Then again, compared to what she had to face in the future, she could handle it.

She could handle anything. It was what she did. Capable Callie. Canny Callie. No one ever saw lonely, emotionally fragile Callie, a woman who craved love and affection and a foolproof guarantee that she wouldn't end up like her mum.

'Damn,' she muttered, swiping a final slick of lip gloss across her lips and staring wide-eyed at the mirror so she wouldn't cry.

She didn't like feeling edgy, as if she'd snivel at any moment. Considering their impending goodbye she'd have plenty of time for that tomorrow.

Until then...*time to put her game face on.*

Archer held onto Callie's hand through the ceremony, the congratulations, and most of the reception.

He caught her wary glances several times and squeezed her hand in response, as if he never wanted to let go.

The truth was he was absolutely freaking terrified.

Weddings scared him.

The Fletts *en masse* scared him.

Combine the two? Guaranteed scare-fest.

Thankfully, having Callie meet his family at the barbecue and on the beach guaranteed he was safe from his mum's matchmaking for once. But holding onto her hand was more than a gesture, and only he knew it.

She anchored him.

Her ability to socialise with ease, to smile and laugh and be absorbed by his family's mayhem, to make everyone around her feel at ease, was a gift.

Maybe it was all the romantic claptrap in the air? Maybe it was Christmas working its magic? Whatever it was, he found himself strangely reluctant to let her go.

And not just her hand.

Even now, after she'd survived the Flett females' incessant teasing when she caught the bouquet, after dancing with Izzy and the kids until she hobbled, after being ribbed by his brothers, she stood tall, surrounded by the bride, the bridesmaids and his mum, laughing and exuberant and glowing.

She'd never looked so beautiful.

It was more than her brown hair hanging in a sleek curtain down her back, her lush lips slicked in gloss the same colour as her dress, her bare shoulders glittering with a dust of bronze.

It was *her*.

When they'd met in Capri she'd blamed her spontaneity on her Italian heritage and he'd loved her impulsiveness. But it was more than that. She was alive in a way many people weren't. People who dragged their bored butts to work every day, doing a job they hated to pay the bills, returning to equally dead-end relationships at the end of a day.

By the way Callie glowed she'd never had a boring day in her life.

What would it be like to be close to that vitality on a daily basis? Would it rub off?

He loved his life, loved the constant travelling and challenges and business success, but he'd be kidding himself if he didn't admit some of the gloss had worn off lately. Now that he wasn't competing as much he felt jaded, as if his lifestyle wasn't all it was cracked up to be.

Having someone like Callie along for the ride would brighten his days, that was for sure. But with her mum terminally ill would she go for it?

'That's some young lady you've lucked in with.'

His dad sidled up to him and Archer inadvertently braced for another confrontation.

'No such thing as luck, Dad. It's the legendary Flett charm.'

Frank's tentative guffaw sounded as if he had something stuck in his throat. Probably his conscience.

'Whatever it is, she's a keeper.'

'Thanks. I'll take your advice into consideration.'

Archer silently cursed his hint of sarcasm when Frank stiffened, hesitated as if weighing his words.

'Don't let her get away,' he said.

Archer swallowed his annoyance at being given relationship advice from a father who'd deliberately shut him out years ago.

Frank cleared his throat. 'We worry about you, son.'

Yeah, right. His dad was so worried that despite the times he'd made tentative overtures these last few years he'd been brushed off or shut down every time.

'Don't. I'm having the time of my life.' Archer made the *shaka* sign. 'Living the dream.'

Frank's scrutiny almost made him squirm. 'Are you?'

'Hell, yeah.' His response came too quickly, sounded too false. 'I like what I do. It's better than—'

He bit back the rest of what he'd been going to say, on the verge of saying more than he should.

'Better than what?' Frank swept his arm wide. 'Better than being stuck near your family?'

Archer took a steadying breath. Another. 'Do you really want to do this here? Now?'

Frank shook his head, sorrow deepening the creases around his eyes. 'I've only ever wanted what's best for you.'

Archer knew he should walk away now. Make a flippant remark to cover his profound anger and walk away.

But he'd had a crappy day, he was confused about Callie, and he'd had a gutful of being on the outside with his dad for leading the life he did.

'What's best for me is staying true to myself. What about you, Dad? What's best for you?' Years of suppressed anger and pain bubbled up and he couldn't have stopped the questions even if he'd wanted to. 'Having your family around you while you battle a life-threatening illness? Being able to rely on your sons to take care of business while you're juggling chemo? Trusting your family to support you no matter how ill you feel or how bad the diagnosis?'

Frank recoiled as if he'd struck him, but Archer wasn't finished.

'I saw you, Dad, that day you finally told me about being given the all-clear.' He sucked in a breath. The vision of that day was embedded deep, yet so clear. 'Eighteen freaking months too late, you finally deemed me responsible enough to handle the truth about your prostate cancer. After I stormed out you sat at the piano, slid your sheet music into a folder, and you cried. You sobbed like you'd been given a death sentence rather than the all-clear. And right then I knew how big a battle you must've faced, and it acted like a kick in the guts all over again.'

Hating how his voice had clogged, he lowered his tone. 'You should've told me earlier, Dad. I should've been here!'

'You're wrong.' Frank stared at him as if he were a stranger. 'I cried because I knew I'd done the right thing in not telling you, despite how damn furious you were. Even though seeing you hurting almost killed me more than the bloody cancer.'

Stunned at his dad's words, Archer pinched the bridge of his nose. It didn't help ease the headache building behind his eyes.

'You still think you did the right thing in not telling me—?'

'Son, you were a world champion when I finally told you. You'd done it. Followed your dream. Achieved the ultimate. I was so proud of you.'

Frank blinked, and the sight of possible tears tempered Archer's disbelief like nothing else.

'That's what I wanted for you. Success. It kept me going all through the illness: watching your competitions, charting your stats, following every mention on the internet. It gave me focus even when I felt like giving up.'

Frank gripped his arm and gave it a little shake.

'*You* did that. You helped me in ways you can't possibly imagine. And no way in hell would that have happened if you'd known about the cancer.'

Shock peppered every preconception about his dad Archer had ever had, and he couldn't formulate a word in response.

Frank gestured towards the family. 'As much as I love those guys, and the support they gave me, their constant hovering became smothering.' His rueful grin eased the lines bracketing his mouth. 'Some days I'd fake fatigue just so I could get into bed with my laptop and check out what you'd been up to.'

'Hell, Dad.' Archer dragged a hand through his hair, wanting to say so much but still floundering.

'Did you know I could've toured with the Melbourne Symphony Orchestra?'

Whiplashed by the change of topic, all Archer could do was shake his head.

'I would've liked performing to large crowds, living on the road.' Frank squared his shoulders and gazed fondly at his wife. 'But I met your mother and my dreams changed. I ended up teaching local kids and looking forward to your mother's slow-cooked lamb and apple pie and long walks along the beach every night.'

His dad rested his hand on his shoulder.

'While I don't regret staying in Torquay and giving up on my dream, I didn't want you to give up yours, son. I wanted you to have the chance I never had.'

Stunned, Archer stared at his dad—really looked at him for the first time in years. 'That's the real reason you didn't tell me?'

Bashful, Frank nodded. 'I'm sorry for being a jerk at the surf school yesterday. The distance between us over the years has been rough. We both have too much pride for our own good. And the bigger the divide between us the guiltier I felt about what I'd done, and the harder to breach the gap became. Then I saw you re-bonding with everyone and I wanted to do the same, but things were so damn awkward between us all the time. I just didn't know how to express half of what I was thinking.'

'Honestly, Dad, I don't know what to say.' Archer blew out a long breath, knowing he had to exorcise the past and move forward. 'I tried a few times but you always shut me down, pretended nothing was wrong. Now you tell me all this stuff and I'm having a hard time dealing with it.'

'Deal with it. Move on. Life's too short.' Frank nodded towards the dance floor, where the mayor was treading on his mum's toes for the umpteenth time. 'I'm happy with the life choices I've made.'

What about you?

Though his dad didn't say it, the question was there, lurking in his shrewd stare.

Archer had led a charmed life. No regrets.

A peal of laughter floated on the air and he turned, seeing Callie as if in slow motion, with her head thrown back, her hair streaming behind her. Her laughter was loud and boisterous and genuine, and he could have sworn his heart turned over.

He'd lied. He did have one regret in his life. Walking away from this incredibly striking woman.

The real question was, would he make the same mistake twice?

'Settling down isn't all bad.' Frank's genuine smile alleviated the tension between them. 'Happens to the best of us. Just ask your brother.'

Archer winced as he saw Travis doing the Time Warp with his bride. Trav gawky and awkward, Shelly laughing so hard she clutched her sides.

'Think about what I've said, son.' Frank nodded towards Callie, who glanced up at that moment and waved. 'You'd be a fool to let a woman like that slip through your fingers for the sake of a footloose, fancy-free lifestyle. Times change and so do we. We move with them or get left behind.'

As Callie moved towards them, Frank chuckled and nudged him in her direction.

Archer didn't know what to think. His head was spin-ning with what he'd learned; his heart was reeling from the possible truth.

Did he dare give up one dream to trust his heart and follow another?

CHAPTER TEN

'I've never had a Christmas like this,' Callie said, staring at the table in amazement.

Covered in crisp white linen, crimson tealights, vases filled with decorative baubles, sparkling crystal, shiny silverware and tiny handmade wreaths sprinkled with silver glitter, it stretched from one end of the marquee to the other.

'Trav and Shelly wanted a combined Christmas-wedding theme, but I think Mum commandeered the decorations.' Archer pointed overhead at the liberal mistletoe hanging from strategically placed hooks. 'She's always gone the whole hog with Christmas. It's the same every year.'

'It's beautiful.' Callie cleared her throat, embarrassed by the sudden surge of emotion making her want to cry. 'You're lucky.'

He must have caught her hint of whimsy and he clasped her hand. 'How do you usually celebrate?'

'Low-key,' she muttered, instantly ashamed of her bitterness.

She'd tried to take her mum on day-trips, especially on special occasions like birthdays and Christmas, but Nora had deteriorated so fast over the last few years it had become easier to stay in.

Her mum had been so distressed last Christmas that she'd made Callie promise not to do it again.

So celebrations these days consisted of snuck-in take-away Thai and luscious chocolate cake from Brunetti's, carols on her iPod and a lot of forced cheerfulness when neither of them really felt like celebrating.

Even their gifts had gone the way of practical rather than indulgent. That hadn't stopped her buying an e-reader Nora could swipe with a fingertip, special organic cream for her crêpe-like skin, and her favourite chocolates this year.

She'd ordered online a few days ago, when she'd been flushed with happiness after her escapades with Archer at the beach.

If she was going to live in the moment, she wanted her mum to also.

Now, with her heart deliberately sealing itself off and her impending departure in the morning, she wondered if she'd been foolish and frivolous.

'Guess it's hard celebrating when your mum's so sick.'

'Yeah.'

He stared at her with blatant curiosity and she wished she'd kept her mouth shut. What better way to ruin their last evening together than to rehash her dysfunctional family's past? Especially in the face of his familial warm and fuzzy perfection.

'You don't want to talk about it?'

She shot him a grateful smile. 'I'd rather focus on this.'

She waved towards the table as the first guests trickled in from the other entry. 'It's really beautiful.' On impulse, she kissed him on the cheek. 'Thanks for coercing me into accompanying you to this wedding.'

He had the grace to look sheepish. 'Sometimes a guy's gotta do what a guy's gotta do.'

That motto applied to girls too, and for tonight she'd drink, dance and be merry. And later, she'd spend an incredible night in Archer's bed, hoarding away memories she'd always cherish.

She hadn't had the opportunity last time, had deliberately banished their time together courtesy of his abrupt break-up. And she'd had more important things to worry about since, like her mum's illness.

Yet for all her reservations about getting involved with him again this week she was glad she'd done it. The last seven days had shown her that the guy she'd thought she'd known in Capri she hadn't known at all. Archer was caring and intuitive, and he had vulnerabilities like the rest of them, and discovering his hidden depths had guaranteed she fell for him.

That was another thing she was glad she'd done: confronting him with her feelings. While she still wished things could have been different, the outcome wasn't unexpected. How could a guy who'd been emotionally shut off from his family for years commit emotionally to her, when realistically they'd known each other for only two weeks eight years apart?

'There is a way you can thank me properly.'

'How?'

He slid an arm around her waist and tugged her close. 'Look up.'

'Beautiful hand-crafted wood beams, red-gum panelling—'

'Mistletoe,' he murmured, a second before he kissed her—a ravishing, soul-reaching melding that left her breathless and clinging to him when he eased away.

It was only then that she registered the hoots and claps of the Fletts.

She blushed, while Archer waved towards the clan,

squared his shoulders and escorted her to pride of place
with the rest of the family at the head of the table.

As he pulled out her chair and caressed the back of
her neck, a sliver of longing lodged in her shielded heart.

What would it be like to belong to a family like this? To
be surrounded by love and laughter? She'd never known
it, and she'd never felt her deprivation so acutely as now.

Her dad had done that to her—taken away any semblance of a happy family upbringing—and while she'd
given up on him a long time ago it was moments like these
when she could easily throttle Bruno Umberto.

She could thank him for her dark hair and eyes, her love
of pasta and her quick-fire temper, but there was little else
Bruno deserved her gratitude for.

The self-absorbed man who'd now married four times,
who lived life on the edge and loved the same way, had
breezed in and out of her life like a flitting butterfly.

Since Nora had been diagnosed he hadn't been near
them, and the odd e-mail didn't cut it.

The genetic testing had proved she hadn't inherited the
mutated gene from her mum. Luckily she hadn't inherited
something far more deadly from her father.

His selfishness.

She'd be there for her mum whatever it took, whatever
she had to sacrifice, however much it hurt.

'You're kinda spaced out.' He waved a hand in front of
her face. 'Everything okay?'

She dredged up a dazzling smile to fool him. 'Fine.'

She'd ensure everything was fine tonight, for come tomorrow their dalliance would be over. But for a fleeting
moment she wished she had Bruno's selfish streak and
could demand this wasn't the end.

'Hey, surf dude, when are you going to introduce us?' A

tall, broad-shouldered guy who had the Flett blond good-looks sat next to Archer and jostled him.

Archer grinned and elbowed him back. 'Callie, this is my cousin Jonesy.' He draped a proprietorial arm across the back of her chair. 'Jonesy, this is my friend Callie.'

'You're a stunner.' Jonesy reached across Archer and shook her hand vigorously, his smile goofy rather than leery.

'Thanks,' she said, grateful when Jonesy started interrogating Archer about wave conditions for the upcoming season.

Friend.

He'd introduced her as his friend, and while it might be the truth it sounded so distant after what they'd shared.

All her one-on-one pep talks with her voice of reason meant nothing in the face of reality.

Mistletoe kisses, passionate love in the sand dunes and cuddles on the balcony aside, she was right back to where she'd been in Capri.

Wishing for a miracle.

Wishing for him to love her.

After what she'd been through with her mum, she'd given up on miracles a long time ago.

What could be so different now?

But she wouldn't waste her life pining. She'd move on ASAP.

Starting first thing in the morning.

Archer couldn't figure it out. One minute Callie had been kissing him with all the passion and exuberance he'd come to expect from her, the next she'd retreated.

Not that it was obvious to anyone but him. She danced and giggled and ate two pieces of red velvet wedding cake, apparently having a ball.

But he could tell. Every time she glanced his way he saw the shadows. Fleeting, willow-o-the-wisp flickers of… what? Pain? Regret? Disappointment?

He'd wanted to ask what was wrong on their drive home, but she'd been trying hard to fill the awkward silence, chatting non-stop about his family and the ceremony and the exchanging of gifts. And he'd been happy to let her talk, still trying to assimilate the truth behind his dad's secrecy all those years ago.

He'd wanted to thank her for encouraging him to swallow his pride and give his family a go, for making him see beyond his anger and resentment. But she hadn't stopped talking. Anything to avoid silence.

Yeah, there was definitely something wrong. Or maybe she just felt weird about their impending departure tomorrow?

Not that she should. He had it all figured out. Make tonight a night to remember, wake up with her in his arms Christmas morning, then talk to her when they arrived back in Melbourne.

He had a rough plan that he'd come up with over the last few hours.

His dad was right. His pushy brothers were right.

Callie was a keeper.

He'd be a fool to let her go.

He hadn't figured out all the logistics yet. He'd never done a long-distance relationship. Hopefully with a little help from her they'd figure out how this would work.

The thought of having her in his life made him want to ditch the tux, grab his board and head for the beach—but to celebrate, not to escape. He wanted to crest a wave, ride a tube, to see if anything could beat the adrenalin rush of realising he didn't have to lose Callie.

Not this time.

'I know you said no gifts, but I've got you something,' she said, strolling towards him on the balcony before sliding onto the love seat next to him.

He shook his head. 'Should've known you wouldn't listen,' he said, wondering what she'd think of his gift when he presented it to her tomorrow.

He'd arranged it online ten minutes ago, as part of his grand plan, while she'd been 'turning back into a pumpkin'—her words, not his—exchanging her dress and up-do for T-shirt, leggings and a loose ponytail that left tendrils curling around her face.

She looked tousled and tired and casual, and she'd never looked so beautiful.

'It's nothing big. I brought it with me. Didn't want to be caught empty-handed. It's not much.'

She was bordering on babbling, and he covered her hand with his to calm her. 'It's from you. I'll love it.'

Darting a nervous glance at him, she gnawed on her bottom lip, her nerves puzzling. It was only a gift. Then again, considering the yearning he'd glimpsed when his family were handing out gifts after the wedding, and the way she'd clammed up about her family celebrating the Christmas holidays, he figured maybe presents were a big deal for her.

He took his time, tugging on the gold ribbon, fiddling with the knot, sliding his finger under the sticky-tape.

'Hurry up,' she said, practically squirming with impatience.

'I see you're a rip-it-off-in-one-quick-move girl,' he said, putting her out of her misery by tearing the paper in three broad strips to reveal something that snatched his breath with the same surreal, suffocating sensation he'd had being caught in a rip once.

'What—? How—?'

He remembered the day they'd stumbled upon the tiny glassblower's cottage as if it was yesterday. It had been their third day together in Capri—a day filled with swimming in a pristine ocean, sharing grilled calamari and fresh bread for lunch, indulging in a decadent session of afternoon delight, before strolling hand in hand through the cobbled streets.

They'd laughed and jostled and snuggled, typical holiday lovers, and discovering the cottage with exquisitely made glass figurines had made Callie's day. She loved that kind of thing, and he'd indulged her by going in, surprised by the wizened old guy who looked about a hundred creating mini-masterpieces.

The porpoises had caught his attention because he'd seen some during his first major competition, and he'd labelled them his good luck charm ever since.

He'd commissioned a Californian artist to carve a replica of these little glass guys a few years ago, and it took pride of place in the entry hall of his Malibu home.

A home that, like the rest of them, he barely visited.

'You thought it was cool when we went into that glassblowing shop in Capri, so I went back and bought it. I was going to give it to you that last day, but...' She trailed off, not needing to finish.

He'd acted like a jackass, deliberately saying stuff he didn't mean before he let another person get close. Easier to depend on no one and avoid the ultimate let-down.

'Reading too much into a holiday fling...nothing more than a bit of fun...lighten up before you scare off more guys.'

The words came back to haunt him. Come tomorrow he'd make amends and say the words she wanted to hear.

He had all night to work on his delivery. When he wasn't making love to her, that was.

'I was a jerk.'

'Yeah, but you were right.'

He didn't like her emotionless tone, or her shuttered expression as he turned over the delicately intertwined frolicking porpoises.

'I can't believe you've kept them all these years.'

She ran a fingertip along their fins, a soft, wistful sigh escaping her lips. 'I actually forgot I had them. Then, when you showed up and bossed me into coming here, I thought they'd make an okay Christmas gift.'

'An okay gift?' He stared at her in disbelief. Was she being deliberately blasé or did this really not mean anything to her?

She'd kept something so special all these years, something he'd specifically wanted, and she was acting as if she'd given him a pair of woollen socks.

'It's a trinket from the past. Nothing more.'

She shrugged, and the first fingers of doubt crept around his dream of a relationship and strangled it.

'I'm glad this time we had the foresight to know this was a fling and nothing more. No expectations that way. No feelings get hurt. Nice and clean.'

Her brittle laugh set him on edge.

'What did you say back then? A short time and a good time?' She interlaced her fingers through his. 'It's certainly been that, Archer Flett. Consider this a thank-you gift too.'

Gobsmacked, he let her take the porpoises and place them on the glass-topped table beside them before clambering onto his lap. Her arms snaked around his neck, tugging his head towards her, her lips meeting his in an explosion of need.

There was nothing tender about the kiss. It was pure desperation, heat and passion and fear. Fear of the future? Fear of farewell?

Whatever, now wasn't the time to dwell on it. He had a million questions to ask her.

In the morning.

For now he wanted to show her how much she meant to him.

He might not be able to eradicate the immature stuff he'd said in Capri, but he could sure as hell let his actions do all the talking now.

CHAPTER ELEVEN

CALLIE wasn't proud of what she'd done.

She should have told Archer the truth last night. And she shouldn't have snuck away in the early hours. Or made Tom complicit in her deceit.

She had to give him credit for not spilling her secret. She'd half expected Archer to confront her about her plan to abscond once she'd asked Tom for a favour at the wedding.

But Archer hadn't suspected a thing.

She'd had her chance to say goodbye and she'd taken it. Several times during the night, with each erotic encounter surpassing the last.

It had been subliminal, knowing it would be their last time together. She'd imprinted every whispered word, savoured every caress, treasured every touch.

If Archer had been surprised by her wild enthusiasm he hadn't shown it. He'd responded in kind, taking her to heights she'd only ever read about in novels.

And then she'd left, creeping out at 5:00 a.m.

Thankfully Izzy had been asleep in the back of the car, and after a few less than subtle questions Tom had given up interrogating her.

The Fletts were a loyal bunch, for not once had Tom

discredited his brother, apart from saying he was a nong for letting her get away again.

She'd had to give him something to shut him up, so she'd settled for a semi-truth. They'd already said their goodbyes last night. They were happy to resume their respective lives, and she had to get back to her mum on Christmas Day.

All perfectly respectable, perfectly legitimate reasons... for running out like a chicken.

The truth was she couldn't face the long car ride back to Melbourne with Archer—couldn't face the awkwardness of another goodbye.

This way they could resume their old relationship—e-mailing for business—and avoid any mess.

He was flying out today, so he wouldn't have time to worry about her early departure anyway. He had things to do, places to be.

Things and places that didn't include her.

That was why she'd given him the porpoises. She'd lied about that too, telling him she'd forgotten about them.

As if. She might have banished her memories of their time in Capri, but every now and then, when her mum had a particularly bad day and Callie felt lonely, she'd take them out of their recycled cardboard box, cradle them in her hand and remember...

Remember that special time in Capri, wishing she could have one ounce of it again.

Well, now she had, and where had it left her? Worse than before. Seriously in love with a guy who had no clue.

To his credit, his reaction to her gift had blown her away. She hadn't expected to see him emotional, and for a few tense moments beforehand had half expected him not to remember that day in Capri at all. But he had. And it had made her wish things could be different all the more.

Instead she'd go back to working on his lucrative campaigns—with the bonus of having Nora's medical bills taken care of—and he'd hit the surf on some exotic island far removed from Melbourne and the memories they'd built.

Memories that would have to last a lifetime.

For now, it has time to get on with her life, starting with a quick visit to Rivera's to wish Artie a Merry Christmas and then spending the day with her mum.

The Spanish bar was jumping when she arrived, with revellers in Santa hats and flashing reindeer noses spilling out onto the street. Many locals came straight from mass to get a taste of Artie's special virgin sangria on Christmas morning, before heading off to their respective hot roast lunches with family.

It had become a Johnston Street tradition, and one she enjoyed, because it gave her an all too brief taste of what a normal Christmas should be.

Not like the understated days she'd had growing up, where she'd wait for her dad to show up with the pony he'd promised only to be disappointed yet again.

Or the recent Christmases spent with Nora, forcing cheer when all she'd felt like doing was holding her mum fiercely and banishing the disease slowly sapping her life.

She slipped through the crowd and entered the main door, her despondency lifting when she glimpsed Artie taking pride of place behind the bar, his costume this year more outlandish than the last.

He'd gone for monstrous reindeer antlers that threatened to take a person's eye out when he turned, a big red nose made from a dyed tennis ball, and a fake white beard that reached to his belly.

It made her happy to see him enjoying life, a far cry

from the devastated man he'd been following his wife's death.

He caught sight of her and waved, calling her over.

Determined to put on a brave face, she wound her way towards the bar, where he swept her into a bear hug.

'*Hola, querida.* Merry Christmas.'

'Same to you.' When he released her she tweaked his nose. 'How can you breathe with that thing?'

'I can't,' he said, in a fake nasally voice, and she laughed. 'Come. Have some sangria.'

For a moment she wished it was the alcoholic version, despite the hour.

'Tell me about this new business.'

Great. Just what she felt like. Talking about her week in Torquay. *Not.*

He poured her a drink, garnished it with a strawberry, slid it across the bar and winked. 'And tell me more about this old *amor.*'

She remembered contradicting Artie a week ago. *I don't love him.*

This time she didn't have the energy to lie.

'The business is exciting. I've developed an online marketing campaign for his new surf school, including online forums and interactive sessions on his webpage, and a social networking page unlike anything anyone's ever seen.'

'Sounds impressive.' Artie topped up her glass even though she hadn't taken a sip. 'Now, tell me about when you weren't working.'

She blushed and Artie patted her cheek, his smile indulgent.

'You're in love. I can tell.'

'How?'

'You have the look.' He pointed at her eyes. 'You have a

sparkle dampened by sadness.' Artie frowned. 'This *amor*, he broke your heart, *si*?'

'No, nothing like that.'

More like she'd broken her own heart by being foolish enough to fall in love despite knowing the expiration date on their seaside fling, knowing he couldn't emotionally commit, and knowing he had traits of her dad she'd rather forget.

Artie cupped his ear. 'You want to talk about it? I'm a very good listener.'

'Don't I know it?'

Artie had listened to her deepest fears and regrets after their unofficial support group for two had formed. He'd been just as forthcoming in his sorrow, yet strangely this time she didn't want to talk about Archer.

Besides, what was there to say? They were headed in different directions, their lives on different paths, without a hope of colliding.

Artie snapped his fingers. 'I can see you don't want to talk to an old man about your *amor*. I understand.' He shrugged. 'If you do, you know where to find me.'

'Thanks,' she said, making a big show of drinking the refreshing fruit sangria as he was called away, when in fact her favourite Christmas drink had already lost its fizz.

With Artie shooting her concerned glances in between mixing drinks and plying his customers with Christmas cookies, she sculled her sangria and gave him the thumbs-up sign.

She had to leave. Before she took him up on his offer to listen. For she had a feeling once she started talking about her relationship with Archer she wouldn't stop.

* * *

Archer stared at the note in disbelief.

> Sorry to run out but had to get back to Mum.
> Tom & Izzy heading to Melbourne to visit Izzy's mum, who unexpectedly dropped into town today so I hitched a ride.
> Thanks. Had a lovely time at the wedding.
> Will be in touch about the surf school campaign when needed.
> Merry Christmas!
> Callie

'What the—?' He slammed his palm on the kitchen benchtop, barely registering the pain of hitting marble so vigorously.

His first instinct was to punch something. The second to grab his board and hit the surf.

He settled for pacing. It didn't help. After several laps of the balcony he flung himself onto the soft-cushioned couch where he'd once sat with Callie and uncurled his fingers to reveal her crumpled note.

He reread it, no closer to understanding.

She sounded so cool, so remote, so untouchable after all that had happened over the last week. They'd reconnected on so many levels, to the point where he'd been about to reveal his thoughts for the future to her this morning.

Schmuck.

This was his family all over again.

Trusting someone with his heart, only to have them hand it back with a *Thanks, not this time, maybe another,* and having no clue as to why.

To make matters worse it catapulted him back years, to when his family had first told him the truth. The same insidious doubts were creeping in, making him wonder what the hell was wrong with him that the people he trusted the most with his feelings didn't return the favour.

How could she up and leave without saying goodbye? Leaving a freaking note?

He glared at the offending piece of paper in disgust, bitterness twisting his gut into knots.

Growling in frustration, he shoved it in his pocket and headed for the storage room under the house where he stashed his gear. He had to hit the waves. It was the place he did his best thinking.

However, as he stomped around, grabbing a wetsuit and his favourite board—the one with more dents than a dodgem—a funny thing happened.

Some of his initial anger faded, to be replaced by a clarity that left him shaken.

He paused mid-step, halfway between the storage room and his car.

What the hell was he doing?

It was Christmas morning—a time for warmth and caring and happiness. Emotions he'd been lacking lately, if he were honest with himself.

Not this last week with Callie, but before that.

Riding the tubes hadn't held the same buzz in a long time, crashing in fancy hotel rooms after a competition had lost appeal, and the string of meaningless dates left him feeling faintly empty.

The real reason behind the surf school had been to make his family sit up and take notice, see he was more than a sport-obsessed surfer, to show them they'd done wrong in not trusting him with his dad's illness.

But another underlying reason was that he'd wanted to give something back to the sport that had given him everything, and connecting with the kids at the beach last week had made him feel worthy in a way he hadn't in for ever.

That had been the hardest thing to realise over the years following his dad's cancer disclosure—that somehow he hadn't been worthy. He might now understand his dad's motivation for secrecy, but it would take a while for his old beliefs to ease.

Hanging with the teens had helped with that. Callie had too. He'd felt rejuvenated this last week, had truly felt close to a woman for the first time ever.

She'd made him reassess the way he treated his family, made him see things in a new light. And he'd been happy in a way he hadn't for a long time. So what the hell had happened?

Buoyed by his overture towards his dad, he'd taken another risk and told her he had feelings for her. Why had she run?

After she'd given him that gift last night he'd thought she felt the same way… Well, he'd thought wrong.

The way he saw it, he had two options. Forget about the gift he'd bought her, then head for the surf before boarding that plane this afternoon and heading back to the life he knew.

Or quit running and confront Callie.

He headed for the car, the board tucked under his arm suddenly weighing him down. When he stowed it in the back, the weight didn't shift. Then his gaze landed on the red Roadster he'd driven Callie here in—a replica of the car they'd explored Italy's south coast with.

He remembered the thrill of taking the curves of a spectacular scenic route, laughing and teasing, and later he'd explored *her* sensational curves in minute detail.

He'd wanted to resurrect the past—this car was testament to that—but was he willing to try a different outcome this time?

What would his life be like if he didn't walk away second time round? If he made a full-blown declaration and truly trusted her with his heart?

Terror made his hands shake, and he stuffed them into the pockets of his board shorts.

He had his answer right there.

He'd re-established a bond with his dad and he'd never felt so relieved. Taking a risk on people wasn't all bad. And he wouldn't be feeling this sick unless he really felt something for Callie. Something that went deeper than caring.

The question was, how far was he willing to go to prove it to her?

Callie had put on a brave face for her mum. She'd made a show of savouring the cardboard-tasting turkey and dry Christmas pud, she'd sung the loudest through the residents' carolling, and she'd fake-laughed over each and every corny joke pulled from a cracker.

She'd thought she'd done a pretty good job of pretending there was nothing wrong. Until she wheeled her mum back to her room and Nora snagged her hand, concern deepening the fatigue lines in her sunken cheeks.

'What's wrong?'

Callie opened her mouth to protest but Nora shook her head.

'Do me a favour, sweetheart, and let me be a mum to you in whatever way I can.'

As a guilt trip, it worked. She'd been taking care of her mum for a while now, and she knew it irked the once independent Nora.

Nora had relished her role as a single mum, not once complaining. When a job had needed doing, she'd got on and done it, so to have her mobility and her dignity curtailed by this dreadful disease… Callie couldn't begin to fathom how awful it must be.

'Work pressures. Nothing major,' she said, not wanting to worry her mum—not today.

Nora had always loved Christmas with all the trimmings: roast turkey and stuffing, trifle, pudding—the works. They'd always had a fresh tree and stuffed stockings, and a day made all the more special by a mother who'd do anything for her only child.

It might have been understated and only the two of them, but it had meant a lot to her mum.

Now those Christmases were in the past, but the least Callie could do was not ruin this Christmas for Nora. Not when she'd already ruined her own.

Nora searched her face, as if seeking the truth, and Callie ducked down to give her an impulsive hug. 'Don't worry, Mum, I'm fine.'

And then she glanced over her mum's shoulder and saw Archer hovering in the doorway.

'What the?'

'Callie?'

She straightened and laid a comforting hand on her mum's shoulder, hoping her glare conveyed what she wanted: for Archer to turn around and leave the way he'd come.

Following her line of vision, Nora slowly swivelled until she too faced Archer.

'Can I help you, young man?'

He hesitated a moment, before squaring his shoulders and stepping into the room. 'I sure hope so, Mrs Umberto.' He held out his hand to her. 'I'm Archer Flett, a friend of your daughter's.'

The way he gently shook Nora's hand eased Callie's anger somewhat. Though she couldn't figure out why she was so angry. Was she upset at him showing up here, or upset at herself for wanting to fling herself at him despite a definitive goodbye?

Well, on her part anyway. It looked as if he hadn't taken too kindly to her brief farewell note.

'Sorry to barge in on you like this, but I need to see Callie before I fly out later today.'

Callie frowned but he blithely ignored her, his dazzling smile deliberately taunting.

'Merry Christmas, by the way,' he said.

He produced a box from behind his back, in crimson shiny paper bound by gold ribbon. 'Not very original, I'm afraid, but if you're anything like your daughter I thought you might enjoy a sweet treat.'

'How thoughtful.' Nora's hands shook as she took an eternity to undo the ribbon and rip the paper.

Callie had to stop from reaching out to help. Not from pity for her mum but the desire to see Archer leave.

'Dark mint, my favourite.'

Nora's grateful smile made Callie's heart ache. She hadn't wanted to tell her mum anything about Archer, and now the rat had left her no choice. Nora would want to know all about the nice young man who knew her favourite chocolates and how he knew and…the rest.

She'd kill him before she sent him packing.

'I hate to intrude, but do you mind if I have a quick word with Callie?'

Nora shot her a quick look—a very perceptive look by the mischievous gleam in her eyes.

'Not at all. Go ahead.' Nora rattled the box. 'And thanks for these. I'll enjoy each and every one.'

'My pleasure.'

His smile was genuine, without an ounce of pity, and Callie grudgingly admired him for it.

'We can talk outside,' she said, with a subtle jerk of her

head towards the door. The last thing she needed was for her mum's gossip radar to prick up. Any *more*, that was.

Callie couldn't figure out what Archer was doing here. She'd given him an easy out with that note, and she'd assumed he'd jump at the chance to fly off into the blue yonder and resume his life.

The last thing she'd expected was to see him rock up here. It made her angsty and uncertain and decidedly edgy.

She'd had this all figured out—end fling; resume working relationship—and now he'd messed that up.

She waited until they'd stepped outside Nora's room before jabbing him in the chest. 'How did you find me?'

Her snappish tone only served to make him lean against the wall, arms folded, grin cocky.

'Not all that difficult. You said you'd be spending the day here, so I checked redial on the phone at the beach house for the number, rang it, discovered where your mum was staying.'

'Nice one, Sherlock,' she muttered, still clueless as to why he was here.

'Actually, I'd make a lousy detective, because I have no clue as to why you ran out on me in the middle of the night.'

'It was early morning. Tom and Izzy were heading to Melbourne, so I thought I'd get a head start on spending Christmas with Mum.'

'Bull,' he said, his grin replaced by thinly compressed lips and an unimpressed frown. 'You couldn't have rung Tom at four a.m. on impulse to hitch a ride, which means you must've organised this last night.'

Why couldn't he be all brawn and no brains?

'Tom's wisely not answering his phone, but I have no doubt you coerced him into aiding and abetting your little escape.' For the first time since he'd shown up a flicker of uncertainty creased his brow. 'I don't get it, Callie. I thought we had something going—'

'*Had* being the operative word.' She shook her head, wishing her heart would stop flipping all over the place and slamming against her ribcage at the thought of him showing up here because he genuinely cared.

No use wishing for the impossible.

Fact: he was still getting on that plane later today.

Fact: whatever he said wouldn't change a thing. They led different lives, a world apart.

Fact: she loved him, and seeing him again only drove the knife in that little bit deeper.

'Look, we had a great time, Arch, but it's over.'

His glare turned mutinous. 'Doesn't have to be.'

He rummaged in his jacket pocket and pulled out a folded piece of paper.

'Here. This was supposed to be your Christmas present.'

When she made no move to take it, he placed it in her hand and curled her fingers around it.

'Go on, take a look.'

More than a little curious, she unfolded the paper and gasped.

A computer printout for an open-ended, first class, round-the-world air ticket.

In her name.

'We've got a pretty good thing going, Cal, I don't want it to end. This way you can join me wherever I am. We can hang out—'

'No.'

She crumpled the paper ticket and let it fall to the floor, her gut spasming with sorrow.

'Don't you get it? I can't just jet off whenever I feel like it. I have obligations.' She jerked a thumb over her shoulder. 'I can't leave Mum and you know that.'

His face fell. 'I thought… Well, I hoped you might want to explore…a…relationship—'

'On your terms?'

Pain lanced her resolve, making her waver. Was she being too harsh? Was she annihilating any chance of a possible future of happiness?

She shook her head. 'If you're so keen to explore what we have, why don't you stick around? Stop running? Commit to something for once in your life?'

A flash of anger sparked his eyes. 'I've committed my life to being the best in the water—'

'Yeah, but what about out of it? What about your family? You can't bear to spend longer than a few days with them once a year. How the hell do you expect to maintain a relationship?'

She knew what she was doing: deliberately sabotaging his attempt at a relationship. Fear clogged her throat at the thought of continuing what they had, growing closer, only to discover he hadn't really changed after all and she'd end up pining and waiting for someone she couldn't rely on. Been there, done that, still waiting for her dad to bring her the T-shirt as a present.

She might have foolishly wished for a happily-ever-after with Archer this past week, but at the time she'd recognised her pie-in-the-sky dream for being just that. That was why she'd indulged in another week-long fling, confident of the end date.

She'd never take the risk of a full-blown relationship knowing she was opening herself up to further heartbreak.

'Just go.'

She expected him to run as he always did. The fact that he was still standing there, a vein pulsing in his neck, shoulders rigid, only served to rile her further.

What was he waiting for?

'I'm not the one running scared this time, Callie. You are.'

Sadness seeped through her, making her want to curl up in a corner and sleep for a century. 'Shows how well you know me. I'm not running anywhere. I can't.' She jerked her head towards Nora. 'And the fact you'd give me an air ticket expecting I'd follow you on a whim proves it.'

Tears prickled at the backs of her eyes. She had to drive him away before she collapsed in a wailing heap in his arms.

'You don't know me and you never will.'

When he didn't flinch, didn't move, her mum called out, '*You* should go, dear.'

Callie did the only thing possible.

She fled.

CHAPTER TWELVE

FOR the second time today Archer wanted to punch something.

Frustration made his head ache as he watched Callie run away from him.

Again.

He should follow her, try to make her understand... His gaze landed on the crumpled plane ticket at his feet and his resolve hardened.

He'd wanted to explore the spark they shared. She'd rejected him.

Best to walk away and not look back.

'Archer? Could you please come in here a minute?'

Great, just what he needed. For her mum to berate him for messing up her daughter's life.

He snatched the ticket off the floor, jammed it into his pocket and entered the room.

'I have a plane to catch—'

'"Later" is what you said.'

The woman before him might have a terminal disease which left her stoop-shouldered and shaky and fragile, but the determination in her intelligent eyes was pure Callie.

He sat on the footstool opposite her wheelchair. 'I'm not comfortable discussing my relationship with Callie.'

'From what I overheard, seems like you're not comfort-able with a relationship period.'

'Harsh.'

Nora's eyebrow rose. 'But true?'

When he opened his mouth to protest, she held up a trembling hand.

'This is none of my business, but if you want a chance with my daughter I recommend you listen.'

He remained mute.

'Good. You want to know why Calista refused your offer?'

He nodded.

'She's scared.'

'Of?'

'It's not my place to tell you, but I think you need to ask her if you want a future together.'

He let out a breath he'd been unaware he was holding, his fingers relaxing from where they'd dug into the foot-stool's leather.

Damn right he'd ask her. If Callie's mum thought he still had a chance, no way would he waste it.

'You might be interested to know that when Calista re-turned from Europe she was glowing. She had a bounce in her step, she smiled constantly, and she hummed Spanish tunes under her breath. Then I was diagnosed and her ex-uberance faded.' Tears glittered in her eyes. 'I hate this disease for doing that to my beautiful Callie.'

Archer didn't handle emotion well, tears least of all, and he sat there like an idiot, searching for the right thing to say and coming up empty.

'Interestingly, when Calista came to see me last week, before her trip away with you, she had some of that old spark back. Which leads me to believe you were more re-sponsible for her post-Europe glow than geography.'

If acknowledging emotions wasn't his forte, discussing them sent him into full-blown panic.

'We shared something special.'

The simple truth, and the right thing to say by Nora's nod of approval.

'My advice? If you want to share that same spark again, don't give up. Go after her. Convince her how you feel. Make her trust you. Trust is everything to my little girl.'

He knew the feeling.

To his surprise, a lump wedged in his throat, and no matter how many times he swallowed he couldn't dislodge it.

'As for her fear of leaving me in case I die—don't worry. I'll fix that.' Nora's smile turned wicked. 'If she doesn't spend some of her time on the road with you I'll threaten to live out my time in the smelly nursing home up the road—the one with roaches the size of rodents—and donate the exorbitant fees she pays for me to stay here to the lost dogs' home.'

The lump of emotion in his throat eased, and his admiration for this feisty woman skyrocketed. 'I'm glad you're on my side.'

She pointed a bony finger at him. 'I'm only on your side because I can see you're head over heels in love with my daughter. Hurt her—you die.'

He laughed. 'Got the message, loud and clear.' He stood and ducked down to kiss her cheek. 'Thanks.'

A faint pink stained her cheeks. 'I may not be around much longer, but while I'm here I'm going to be the best damned mother-in-law you could ever wish for.'

It took him a good sixty seconds to process what she'd said, and by then he'd reached his car.

Him? Head over heels in love? What were the chances?

As for a mother-in-law…that involved marriage…

By the time he'd hit Alexander Parade some of the initial shock had worn off and he found himself heading for Johnston Street.

He needed answers.

Only one woman could provide them.

Callie texted her mum an apology as soon as she pulled into a parking spot at home.

She'd cooled off by the time she'd walked through to the foyer, and had headed back to Nora's room. But when she'd got there she'd seen Archer in the room. It had looked as if her mum was telling him off so she'd left. She hoped Nora had flayed him alive.

The guy didn't have a clue, thinking she could traipse around the world while Nora was stuck in that home dying.

Selfish. Unthinking. *Male.*

She thumped the steering wheel. It did little for the resentment simmering like a dormant volcano. She wasn't footloose like him. She couldn't jump on a plane whenever he snapped his fingers. She wasn't impulsive and selfish. She wasn't her father.

But as her anger faded a sliver of clarity glimmered through. Maybe she was looking at this all wrong. Archer had walked away from her once without looking back. This time he wanted to continue seeing her, to explore a relationship. And, while she didn't want to risk her heart again, she'd been harsh. She'd said some pretty nasty stuff at the end, accusing him of being a shallow, emotionless commitment-phobe.

And what had he done? Gone and copped more from her mum. Not many guys would do that. The Archer she'd once known would have headed to the airport without hesitation.

But this older, more mature Archer wasn't the same

guy he'd once been. He was wiser, more responsive, more willing to see past the end of his surfboard.

And the thing was, if a guy like him had taken a monumental risk in tracking her down to lay his heart on the line should she consider taking a risk too?

Was her lack of trust worth a life of misery in losing the love of her life?

She rested her hands on the steering wheel and her head fell forward, her eyes closed.

She couldn't leave Nora, that was a given, but maybe she could compromise in some way? She wouldn't expect him to wait for her, but the thought of having Archer in her life—to support her, to care for her when the dreaded inevitable happened with her mum—was pretty darn appealing.

She knocked her head repeatedly against her forearms.

Yep, she'd been a fool.

The rev of an engine penetrated her misery, punctuated by three short blasts on a familiar horn. She lifted her head, daring to hope, just in time to see Archer kill the engine of the red Roadster, unclip his seatbelt and vault over the door.

He strode towards her, determination lengthening his strides, and she got out of the car, waiting for him to reach her.

'We're going for a ride and I want you to promise me you won't speak the whole way.' He snagged her hand and tugged.

She resisted. No use giving in too easily. 'As an apology, that sucked.'

She bit back a grin at his comical disbelief.

'*Me* owe *you* an apology?' He shook his head. 'Not. Another. Word.'

This time she let him lead her towards the Roadster,

open the door and buckle her in. His familiar fresh air and sunshine scent wrapped around her like a comforting hug.

She gritted her teeth to stop herself from nuzzling his neck, and curled her fingers into her palm to stop herself reaching for him.

He took a deliberately long time, taunting her, and she almost capitulated. Almost. He straightened, his grin smug, and she wanted to smack that smugness off his face.

As they wound through the heavy Christmas Day traffic she snuck glances at him, her heart giving an extra kick when they locked stares for a long, loaded moment at some traffic lights.

All her mental pep talks to get over him, all her determination to move on, vanished in that one look. The sizzle of heat was invisible yet unmistakable.

She'd never been more thankful when the lights turned green.

Ten minutes later he'd pulled into a rare parking spot in Lygon Street and his intention hit her.

He'd brought her to Melbourne's Little Italy. Was he aiming to soften her up by resurrecting memories of Capri?

They were so past Capri it wasn't funny, and she fully intended to tell him so. But the hint of vulnerability in his questioning gaze caught her completely off guard and she bit back a smartass remark.

She saved it for when they were seated in a tiny trattoria so reminiscent of their favourite place in Capri she half expected Luigi, the owner, to come strutting out to welcome them.

'Can I talk yet—?'

'No.' He made a zipping motion over his lips and proceeded to order: linguine marinara, fresh bread, Chianti.

Their meal.

Yep, he was trying to schmooze his way into getting her

to change her mind. As if a fabulous Italian meal would do that.

She had obligations.

She had responsibilities.

He snuck his fingers across the table, snagged her hand, lifted it to his lips and kissed her knuckles.

She had it bad.

He released her hand and she reluctantly, perversely, snatched it away.

'You can talk soon, but only after you listen first.' She rolled her eyes and he chuckled. 'I had a plan. Wake up next to you Christmas morning, make all your Christmases come at once—' she winced at his corny pun '—and then tell you how I feel.'

Her pulse stuttered, before pounding like a jackhammer.

'But you robbed me of that opportunity and I wanted to run. I was all set to head to the airport early 'til I re-alised something.'

His gaze dropped to her hands, clasped on the table, before slowly raising to eyeball her, and what she saw snatched her breath.

Adoration? Hope? Dared she think it...*love*?

'I figured this time I wanted to run *towards* something and not away from it.'

Some of her resentment melted as she gnawed on her bottom lip, wanting to speak, afraid of saying too much.

'That airline ticket was my lousy way of saying I want to be with you.' He cleared his throat. 'I can't lose you, Cal. Not this time.'

The silence stretched between them and she took it as her cue to speak.

'I can't traipse around the world after you, even if Mum says it's okay.'

He nodded. 'I know. I was thinking maybe I should

stick around for a while—teach classes at the surf school, give back to my home town and the sport that's given me everything.'

Shock ripped apart her carefully constructed defences.

'You're staying in Torquay?'

'If you make it worth my while.' His mouth kicked up at the corners in a cheeky dare, and she could have sworn her heart kicked right back.

Wow.

Renowned nomad and confirmed gypsy Archer Flett was willing to put down roots. For her.

It was what she'd dreamed of—what she would have traded anything for eight years ago. But despite the urge to be selfish for once in her life, grab what she wanted and damn the consequences, she couldn't do it.

Archer was willing to stick around now, but for how long? What about when the going got tough with her mum? What about when they had to live apart for months because of his work commitments and her emotional ones?

Constant pressures on a relationship would wear it down and she'd be right back where she started. Loving Archer, her trust shattered.

'So what do you say? Think you can handle having me in your life?'

Her heart wanted to yell, *Hell, yeah.*

Her mind froze with the implications of losing him. This time around it would be so much worse, because he was willing to give it all up for her.

And she had to push him away.

'I—I can't. I'm sorry.'

She had a second to register his open-mouthed shock before she bolted from the restaurant, dodging a family of boisterous children brandishing crackers and a bedraggled Santa who looked as if he'd been doing overtime all week.

She couldn't head for the car, and both sides of the road were lined with outdoor chairs and tables filled to overflowing with Christmas revellers.

Her hesitation cost her dearly. A hand clamped around her upper arm.

'I've asked the waiter to hold our meal until we've had a little chat. In private.'

She could have struggled, but with people casting concerned glances their way and reaching for their mobile phones she acquiesced to him leading her to the car, where she slouched in the front seat like a recalcitrant child.

'Nora told me you have trust issues and that you'd tell me the rest. Is that what this is about?'

Way to go, Mum, she thought. *Traitor.*

She folded her arms and glared. 'Maybe I'm just not that into you?'

He laughed. 'Not buying it. Try again.'

She clamped her lips shut in the hope that he'd tire of the silent treatment and give up.

'She said you were scared. Has some guy done a number on you? Because I can emasculate him if that'll help.'

The corners of her mouth curved upwards before she could stop them.

'You know I'll keep throwing out outlandish suggestions 'til you tell me the truth, right?'

And he would. If the guy had been determined enough to win the World Championship five times, odds were he wouldn't let up.

She took a deep breath, blew it out. 'My dad let me down repeatedly. Rarely followed through on promises. Popped in when he felt like it. Paid more attention to his next three wives than he did to Mum and me. Then when Mum was diagnosed he stopped contact altogether.'

Archer swore.

'Yeah, I think I've used that expletive a few times my-self.' She shrugged, hoping he'd back off and she wouldn't have to divulge the rest—the real reason why she was pet-rified of a relationship with Archer. 'Guess I'm reluctant to trust people because of that.'

'There's more.'

She should've known he'd be too smart to let this go.

'Cal, look at me.'

But she couldn't. Couldn't risk him seeing her real fear.

'Your dad sounds like a selfish jerk, but that's not what has you so scared.'

When she still wouldn't eyeball him, he swore again. 'Thanks to you, I sorted things out with my family. I stashed my damn pride and took the first step in rebuild-ing the gap I created.' He jabbed a thumb at his chest. 'I've got trust issues too, because they didn't trust me enough to confide in when they should've. I often wonder if it's me, something about me that made them do that. But I'm not wasting time second-guessing myself any more, Cal. It's not worth it. I'm going out on a limb here because it's *you*. I'm scared like you are, so there has to be more.'

Damn him for being so intuitive.

'Is this about the motor neurone disease? Are you scared you'll inherit it?'

Her gaze snapped to his, and in that instant she gave away her final fear.

'Because it's natural to be scared, but whatever hap-pens in the future we'll face it together.'

'Are you crazy? You saw my mum. And she's only going to get worse. You think I want you to…?' She trailed off in horror, tears blurring her eyes at how close she'd come to blurting the truth.

'Tell me.'

He placed a fingertip under her chin and gently tipped it up so she had no option but to look at him.

She wanted to fob him off, to lie, but the love blazing from his intent stare was her undoing.

'You think I want you to be stuck with something like that? For you to give up your freedom for me?' She shook her head, dislodging his touch. 'If the disease didn't kill me, the guilt would.' A great sob tore from her chest. 'I want more for you.'

'*You're* all I want—'

He broke off, and for one horrifying moment she thought he might cry.

'Look, I'm new to this emotional stuff. I don't know what to do or say to prove I love you.'

He dropped his head into his hands, his defeatist posture so far removed from the confident guy she knew it got through to her as nothing else could.

He loved her.

He wanted to be with her.

How many people got a second chance at their first love?

Tentative, she reached out and laid a hand on his shoulder. 'Genetic testing says I don't carry the mutated gene, but that doesn't mean I can't get it. My chances are still elevated.'

He lifted his head, his bleak expression tearing at her inside. 'Life's full of risks, Cal. I take risks every day. Sharks. Rips. Getting on a plane. In a car. If we don't take risks we're half dead anyway. And that's not you. The woman I remember in Capri was vivacious and bold and lived life to the max. I've seen glimpses of that woman the last week and she's magnificent.'

She couldn't speak if she wanted to. Her throat was constricted with emotion.

'I won't pre-empt your mum, but she's going to tell you the same thing I just did. She wants you to make the most of your life, to embrace it, not run from it for fear of losing it one nebulous day that may never come.'

'I don't want you to give up who you are for me. I won't be that selfish, like Dad—'

'He's a callous bastard and you're nothing like him. You're standing by your mum. You're doing everything in your power to show her how much she means to you. As for your trust issues because of him, I can deal with them.' He jabbed a hand through his blond spikes. 'I can deal with anything as long as I have you by my side.'

When it came down to it, that was what convinced her to give their relationship a go.

Having Archer by her side, through good and bad, was a pretty potent attraction.

'What about kids? I'm not sure I could take the risk. They may inherit—'

'Enough. You're reaching for excuses, probably terrified to commit like me.'

Damn straight she was.

He tapped his chest. 'If you're feeling half as vulnerable and open wide in here as I am, you're grasping at whatever you can to avoid taking a risk.'

He was good. He'd homed in on exactly how she was feeling: raw and vulnerable and shell-shocked.

And downright petrified.

He was right. She was grabbing at any old excuse, hiding her fear behind it.

But in opening her heart to him a second time around hadn't she already taken the biggest risk of all?

He snagged her hand, squeezed it. 'You're worrying about the future when we need to live in the present.'

When her mum had been diagnosed, and later when

Callie had been given the all-clear following genetic testing, she'd made it her mission to make the most of every opportunity.

Archer had proved how much he loved her by his willingness to give up what he treasured most: his freedom.

He wanted to be with her for ever. It was the greatest opportunity of a lifetime.

What was she waiting for?

He enveloped her in his arms and she finally let go, her emotion spilling out in torrents of tears as she drenched his shirt.

'Kids, marriage, the works, we'll face it. Together,' he murmured, smoothing her hair, stroking her back until her sobs subsided.

Stunned that this incredible man was willing to give up so much to be with her, she eased back and gazed into his eyes.

'I love you. I always have.'

He kissed her, long and slow.

By the time they made it back to the restaurant their Christmas dinner was cold.

EPILOGUE

'WE SHOULD HAVE eloped to Hawaii,' Archer murmured in Callie's ear after the umpteenth back-slap and congratulatory kiss.

Callie elbowed her new husband. 'And miss out on sharing another Flett Christmas Eve wedding with our families? No way.'

'You're such a romantic sap,' he said, sliding an arm around her waist and holding her close.

'So sue me.' She sighed and snuggled into him. 'Thank you.'

'For?'

'This.'

She waved towards the festivities in full swing on the beach foreshore in front of the Winki Pop Surf School.

Artie, resplendent in tux and Santa hat, was mixing up another batch of his secret sangria.

Izzy, too cute in an eclectic Christmas elf-fairy costume, was racing around Tom in a demented version of Ring-a-Rosie. Travis and Shelly were canoodling, and Archer's folks were sitting hand in hand alongside Nora, watching the fun with benign smiles.

Even the recalcitrant Bruno had made a rare appearance, resurfacing from the Middle East *sans* wife, and trying to make it up to Nora and his daughter.

Let him keep trying. Callie wasn't buying it, even if she'd generously agreed to let him come to the wedding and to Christmas lunch tomorrow.

The wedding ceremony on the beach had been incredible, but it had been earlier, when Archer had carried Nora in his arms and gently deposited her in a front row seat, that Callie had lost it.

He'd wiped away her tears to a chorus of sniffles from their small crowd of guests and she'd managed to hold it together for the vows. Just.

The fact that she'd married her first love, her only love, was so surreal she kept smoothing her strapless calf-length ivory silk wedding dress to ensure it was real.

Lucky for her, Archer rarely released her hand, and his solid presence was all the reassurance she needed.

His gaze followed hers. 'You sure your mum's going to be okay while we honeymoon in Capri? Because I'm happy to stay here—'

'She'll be fine.'

Callie had had a long talk with her mum when she'd almost lost Archer twelve months ago, resulting in her letting go of her residual fears and starting to live life in the moment.

Sure, watching her mum deteriorate a little every day sliced her in two, but Nora was making the most of the time she had left. The least Callie could do was the same.

It was what Nora had wanted—to see Callie happy— and they'd brought the wedding forward for that very reason.

Not that she or Archer minded. They'd been living together anyway, spending Monday to Friday in Melbourne and the weekends in Torquay.

He didn't mind the commute, and she didn't mind a sexy surfer crowding her space. They hadn't decided on permanent living arrangements yet. Time enough when they returned from Capri.

She couldn't believe they were returning to the beautiful town where they'd met, where this amazing guy had wooed her with wine and moonlight and sea.

'What are you thinking?'

She glanced into her husband's deep blue eyes and smiled. 'I'm thinking about old memories of Capri.'

'Well, I'm thinking about creating new ones.'

His exaggerated eyebrow-wiggle made her laugh.

'You know we're going to have an amazing life together, right?' He cradled her face in his hands, his thumbs caressing her cheeks.

'You bet.'

For whatever they faced in the future she'd do it with her incredible husband by her side.

Life didn't get any better than this.

He lowered his head and kissed her, a soft, tender melding of lips that quickly escalated into heat and passion and need.

Maybe it did…

* * * * *

Mills & Boon® Hardback

October 2012

ROMANCE

Banished to the Harem	Carol Marinelli
Not Just the Greek's Wife	Lucy Monroe
A Delicious Deception	Elizabeth Power
Painted the Other Woman	Julia James
A Game of Vows	Maisey Yates
A Devil in Disguise	Caitlin Crews
Revelations of the Night Before	Lynn Raye Harris
Defying her Desert Duty	Annie West
The Wedding Must Go On	Robyn Grady
The Devil and the Deep	Amy Andrews
Taming the Brooding Cattleman	Marion Lennox
The Rancher's Unexpected Family	Myrna Mackenzie
Single Dad's Holiday Wedding	Patricia Thayer
Nanny for the Millionaire's Twins	Susan Meier
Truth-Or-Date.com	Nina Harrington
Wedding Date with Mr Wrong	Nicola Marsh
The Family Who Made Him Whole	Jennifer Taylor
The Doctor Meets Her Match	Annie Claydon

MEDICAL

A Socialite's Christmas Wish	Lucy Clark
Redeeming Dr Riccardi	Leah Martyn
The Doctor's Lost-and-Found Heart	Dianne Drake
The Man Who Wouldn't Marry	Tina Beckett

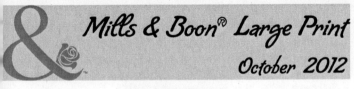

Mills & Boon® Large Print
October 2012

ROMANCE

HISTORICAL

MEDICAL

ROMANCE

A Night of No Return	Sarah Morgan
A Tempestuous Temptation	Cathy Williams
Back in the Headlines	Sharon Kendrick
A Taste of the Untamed	Susan Stephens
Exquisite Revenge	Abby Green
Beneath the Veil of Paradise	Kate Hewitt
Surrendering All But Her Heart	Melanie Milburne
Innocent of His Claim	Janette Kenny
The Price of Fame	Anne Oliver
One Night, So Pregnant!	Heidi Rice
The Count's Christmas Baby	Rebecca Winters
His Larkville Cinderella	Melissa McClone
The Nanny Who Saved Christmas	Michelle Douglas
Snowed in at the Ranch	Cara Colter
Hitched!	Jessica Hart
Once A Rebel...	Nikki Logan
A Doctor, A Fling & A Wedding Ring	Fiona McArthur
Her Christmas Eve Diamond	Scarlet Wilson

MEDICAL

Maybe This Christmas...?	Alison Roberts
Dr Chandler's Sleeping Beauty	Melanie Milburne
Newborn Baby For Christmas	Fiona Lowe
The War Hero's Locked-Away Heart	Louisa George

Mills & Boon® Large Print

November 2012

ROMANCE

The Secrets She Carried	Lynne Graham
To Love, Honour and Betray	Jennie Lucas
Heart of a Desert Warrior	Lucy Monroe
Unnoticed and Untouched	Lynn Raye Harris
Argentinian in the Outback	Margaret Way
The Sheikh's Jewel	Melissa James
The Rebel Rancher	Donna Alward
Always the Best Man	Fiona Harper
A Royal World Apart	Maisey Yates
Distracted by her Virtue	Maggie Cox
The Count's Prize	Christina Hollis

HISTORICAL

An Escapade and an Engagement	Annie Burrows
The Laird's Forbidden Lady	Ann Lethbridge
His Makeshift Wife	Anne Ashley
The Captain and the Wallflower	Lyn Stone
Tempted by the Highland Warrior	Michelle Willingham

MEDICAL

Sydney Harbour Hospital: Lexi's Secret	Melanie Milburne
West Wing to Maternity Wing!	Scarlet Wilson
Diamond Ring for the Ice Queen	Lucy Clark
No.1 Dad in Texas	Dianne Drake
The Dangers of Dating Your Boss	Sue MacKay
The Doctor, His Daughter and Me	Leonie Knight